I0527270

THE BOOK
OF ETERNITY

The Book of Eternity

Jacqueline Pennewill

The Book of Eternity

© 2026 by Jacqueline Pennewill

This is a work of fiction. Unless otherwise indicated, all the names, characters, businesses, places, events and incidents in this book are either the product of the author's imagination or used in a fictitious manner. Any resemblance to actual persons, living or dead, or actual events is purely coincidental.

All rights reserved. No portion of this publication may be reproduced, stored in a retrieval system, or transmitted by any means—electronic, mechanical, photocopying, recording, or any other—except for brief quotations in printed reviews, without the prior written permission of the publisher.

Editors: Deborah Froese, Megan Morris Webb, Noëlla Simmons
Cover and Interior Design: Emma Elzinga

Indigo River Publishing

3 West Garden Street, Ste. 718
Pensacola, FL 32502
www.indigoriverpublishing.com

Ordering Information:

Quantity Sales: Special discounts are available on quantity purchases by corporations, associations, and others. For details, contact the publisher at the address above.

Orders by US trade bookstores and wholesalers: Please contact the publisher at the address above.

Printed in the United States of America

Library of Congress Control Number: 2025908937
ISBN: 978-1-964686-59-2 (paperback)   978-1-964686-60-8 (ebook)

First Edition

With Indigo River Publishing, you can always expect great books, strong voices, and meaningful messages. Most importantly, you'll always find . . . *words worth reading.*

For Mom and Dad who constantly encouraged my creativity and imagination.

Chapter One

Thunder violently shook the earth. Wind tore leaves from the safety of their bending branches, whipping them into a frenzy before sending them tumbling into the darkness.

"You challenge me?" a voice bellowed. The sheer force threw the young man across the forest and impaled him onto a tree branch. Pain shot through him as he lost consciousness. His lifeless body hung limp from the branch.

"How dare you?!" the voice commanded, sending the wind forcefully in the young man's direction, pinning him further.

The young man's head arched back. His eyes opened and immediately turned black. His body floated free from the branch, healing itself. He screamed back into the night as he flew forward only to be thrown back into the tree by the unseen force. The young man's bloodied, broken body slid down the tree and slumped on the ground.

"You are weak," the voice said, disgusted.

Fighting with what little strength he had left; the young man dug his fingers into the dirt and struggled to push himself up. His body was heavy, almost one with the earth. Wind swirled around him. He let out a blood-curdling cry. Finally, too weak and exhausted, he fell to the ground . . . lifeless. The earth slowly groaned. It shook, shifted, until the ground finally split open, revealing a darkness blacker than night. The wind spiraled around the young man's battered body, enveloping it. It lifted him up and casted him viciously into the earthly black hole, closing, leaving no sign of a battle.

"Does anyone else dare challenge me?! I am here before you!" the voice roared from the darkness.

Watchful eyes hid in the darkness. The voice knew there were others reluctant to come forward after what they witnessed. Terrified to reveal themselves, fearing the same fate.

"Come forward. Do not hide in the shadows. No one? I am here. You know what I am capable of! You have witnessed it for centuries . . . but there are still those who want to challenge me! Destruction . . . It is what I live for . . . what I am here for. Fear me or fight me!"

The wind subsided and stopped. The leaves settled.

Silence.

In the darkness of the forest, hidden in the deep, overgrown brush, a black-cloaked figure stood.

"I will challenge you." The figure whispered, raising his head to reveal two glowing yellow eyes under the hooded cloak.

Chapter Two

Grey opened her eyes as the gentle ocean breeze caressed her face. She squinted and adjusted to the bright sun. How long had she been sleeping? She looked out the window as the car approached a big white bridge joining the mainland with Sleepy Key.

"You're awake. Look! Isn't it beautiful?" Mom grinned.

"Hmmm." Grey scowled. She looked around groggily, slowly peeling herself from the hot, vinyl seat. *Another one of her mother's bright ideas,* she thought.

"Where are we?" Grey's twin brother, Michael, pushed himself forward from the backseat.

"We're here," Mom replied.

Grey yawned. "Where's the house?"

"It's over the bridge."

The traffic light on the bridge changed from green to red. All the cars stopped.

"Let's get out." Mom swung the car door open and jumped out.

Grey hesitated for a moment. She closed her eyes and

took a deep breath. She did want to get out and look at the water, but Mom was so chipper, it was enough to make her not want to do it. Reluctantly, she opened the door. Before she stepped out, she could feel the heat rising from the pavement. She raised her hands to shade her eyes from the glare of the sun. It had to be one hundred degrees.

Grey walked over to the bridge railing. She watched small boats float lazily by. A boat horn blared, startling her. A white yacht glided effortlessly through the water, barely making a ripple. The bridge split in half, rising, creating a passageway for the massive boat to move through.

Grey suddenly felt a shove, and quickly grabbed onto the railing of the bridge to stop herself from going over. She turned around to find Michael grinning at her.

"What did you do that for?" Grey asked.

"Because I love my sister." He wrapped his arms around her in a bear hug.

Grey's scowl gave way to laughter. "What made you pick this town, Mom?" Grey asked, struggling to break free from her brother's hold.

"I was looking online for house-sitting jobs in a warm climate for the summer. I saw this wonderful house on the beach," she shrugged. "I thought it would be a fun adventure."

It figured Mom wouldn't research anything, just pick up and go. She had asked Mom what the inside of the house was like before their trip. Mom said she didn't know. When Grey asked if she could get pictures from the owners, she said it didn't matter what the house looked like. What mattered is that they were together. Mom probably didn't have the time, considering she sprang this on Grey and Michael five days before they were leaving.

Michael held his cell phone above his head, waving it around.

"No service." He exhaled loudly.

"Good." Grey walked past him to the other side of the bridge and, just as she was about to peer over the railing, she saw an old white Corvette convertible slowly drive onto the bridge toward her. It stopped behind the other cars.

"Michael," she called.

"What?"

She nodded toward the Corvette.

Michael turned around, his jaw dropping. "Nice car. A 1957 with red interior!"

"Well, if you keep your grades up," Mom said, "you'll be able to buy one of those someday."

"And if I did that, what would we do with Bessie?" Michael asked, patting the roof of the car.

"Come on you two," Mom said as the bridge began to close.

Michael opened the passenger door, lifting the front seat to get in the back. Grey pushed it back into place, plopping into the front seat.

"Don't you make fun of her! I love Bessie!" Mom rubbed the dashboard of the 2004 Honda Accord.

Grey rolled her eyes before she shut the door.

"What? You don't like her either?"

"It's a car, Mom."

"We've been through a lot together. She got us here,

didn't she?"

"Yes," Grey and Michael replied in unison.

Mom and Michael laughed.

Grey turned away, looking out the open car window. *Oh my God. A whole summer of this?* That was another thing that was bothering Grey. She and Michael would turn seventeen this summer, and they weren't home to take their driver's test. When Grey protested, Mom told her she could take the test when they returned home to New Jersey. At the time, Grey was irritated. Now as she stared out the window, it didn't really matter. It wasn't like she would be getting a car anyway.

They continued over the bridge past marinas dotted with white boats and little shops selling summer clothing and knickknacks. Each shop was painted a different pastel color, standing out against the deep, green trees and foliage.

"Okay, where to next Michael?" Mom asked.

"I don't know. No service." Michael waved his phone around. "This is not good, Mom."

"Okay, well I have directions in the glove compartment." Mom sighed. "Grey, would you please get them?"

Grey opened the glove compartment.

"The directions should be right on top," said Mom.

Grey pulled a folded piece of paper from the glove compartment and opened it. "You're supposed to make a left at the next light."

The car turned onto a winding two-lane road with the ocean on the right side and the bay on the left. As they drove, the landscape became dense with tropical foliage. Beautiful flowering bushes were mixed among palm trees, great mighty oaks and other varieties that Grey had never seen before. Everything was so green.

Grey was in awe. The trees were so tall, they formed a canopy above the road. Sunlight peeked through the leaves and the branches, creating a mosaic of light on the road in front of them. Here and there, she caught glimpses of houses dotting the landscape. They were set back on the properties, shrouded in privacy by the surrounding foliage. She found this very intriguing. Some of the homes were newly built gigantic mansions. Others were tiny beach cottages decorated in vibrant colors. They had old, weathered signs in front: Shangri-La and Land of Peace.

"What side is the house on?" Grey asked.

"Oh sure, now you're interested. You could not care less when I told you where we were going to spend the summer," Mom said jokingly.

"Who cares which side the house is on," Michael said. "Look where we are!"

What if they were house-sitting in one of the small homes? Grey would be stuck in close quarters with Mom and her brother all summer. Oh, that would be a nightmare.

"Okay, what number are we looking for?" Mom asked.

"28255," said Grey.

"It's on the oceanside. This is gonna be awesome!" Michael exclaimed.

When they finally saw the numbers 28255 in silver on a shiny red mailbox up ahead, Mom turned into the long driveway. Seashells crunched under the tires. Grey leaned out of her window, gazing up at the huge property. The trees seemed to go up as high as the eye could see. Streaks of sunlight magically found their way through wind-tossed leaves, dancing on the ground.

The car came to a stop at a three story, grey-shingled house. Steps to the far left led up to a shiny red door on the second floor. A two-car garage was tucked underneath the right side of the first floor. A walkway on the left of the garage went through the middle of house, leading out back.

Grey got out of the car and just stood there for a few moments, taking it all in. Something was a little strange, but what was it? Grey looked around, her eyes landing on Michael. It was so quiet . . . and peaceful. Not a bird chirping, not a car passing, nothing.

Michael ran to Mom and hugged her. "This is awesome, Mom!"

Mom laughed.

Grey took a few steps away, admiring the surroundings. As she turned, she saw Mom smiling at her. Grey returned a small smile and looked away. She knew Mom hoped this time away would give them all some time to heal as a family after Dad's death, but Grey just wanted to be left alone. Their relationship was strained, and to Grey, Mom was the enemy.

Michael ran past Grey toward the walkway and disappeared to the back of the house. "Woo hoo! You are never gonna believe this!" he yelled from the backyard, his voice breaking the silence.

Grey and Mom laughed. Grey didn't understand how she and Michael could be so different. Michael was always the positive one, while Grey always questioned things. Being

8

twins, Grey thought they would have something in common, but she never saw any similarities. Michael was popular and good at everything; Grey was shy and unsure of herself. She did have friends, but she was never quite sure why they were friends with her. Was it because of her brother?

One girl pretended to be her friend just to get to Michael, going as far as inviting her on the family vacation to Bermuda. The girl started a social media page dedicated to the ruse, and it seemed everyone knew about it but Grey. It was a good thing Michael found out about it before she could say yes because the girl planned to continue posting during the whole Bermuda trip and the joke was on Grey. She was so embarrassed by the whole experience. The rejection still stung when she thought about what had happened. Locking herself in her room, Grey deleted all her social media accounts and cried until Dad finally got her to open the door.

Grey aways felt close to Dad. The last five years of his life, she grew even closer to him. He always seemed one step away from death. She grasped for who he was before he got sick, because to her, he disappeared a little bit every day. He was always so strong until his cancer made him vulnerable. She hated Dad's cancer more than the girl who had invited her to Bermuda. She was so angry at it for taking him away.

Mom was a free spirit with a carefree confidence. Grey secretly aspired to this but also struggled with it because she didn't know where to begin. Grey thought this was why Mom was able to deal with Dad's illness and death in such a calm manner. Grey couldn't completely grasp Mom's apathy, and this lack of understanding angered her.

"So, what do you think?" Mom asked, putting her arm around her shoulder.

Grey stiffened.

"It's beautiful," Grey said, admiring the surroundings.

Mom smiled.

"Come on, what are you waiting for?" Michael stood in the walkway. "You have to see this!"

Grey and Mom followed Michael through the walkway, and, as they got closer to the end, they heard the faint sounds of the calm ocean and gentle waves breaking along the shore.

Grey stepped out back, standing on the sprawling, teak deck with an in-ground pool at the end. A swing hung very still off to the right corner, and four lounge chairs were lined up at the edge along with a fire pit surrounded by pillows. The stairs to the right led up to the second deck furnished with a large glass table and wrought iron chairs that were centered in an open area in front of French doors.

"We can eat out here every night!" Michael said full of enthusiasm.

Grey looked up to the third level. A deck and another set of French doors piqued her curiosity.

"Let's unpack the car and get everything in the house," Mom said.

Chapter Three

Grey struggled with her suitcase up the long flight of steps. "We could use an elevator." Grey's breathing became heavy.

"Maybe you shouldn't have brought so much stuff." Michael bounded up the steps past her.

"Be quiet!" Grey stopped on the stairwell to catch her breath. She was annoyed at herself for packing so much stuff.

"This is like living in a tree house!" Michael looked around with a big smile, taking in the view.

"It is, isn't it?" Mom passed Grey on the steps.

Grey laughed. She really did love her brother, but did he have to be so damn positive about everything?

Mom put the key in the lock, taking a deep breath. She turned the knob, her eyes crinkling at the corners. What waited for them beyond the red door? Before Mom could move out of the way, Michael pushed past her, almost knocking her over with his suitcase and ran in the house.

"Michael!" Grey complained.

Grey walked in, pulling her suitcase alongside her,

followed by Mom. The inside seemed to be as incredible as the outside! A sprawling living room with a marble fireplace and a wall of windows that lined the front of the house was to their right. Beyond the living room was the massive kitchen with brushed silver cabinets and matching appliances. To the right of the kitchen was the dining room with French doors that opened out onto the second level of the deck and a view of the deep blue waters. Grey had forgotten for a moment that the house was on the water. *Imagine eating and getting to see the ocean too.*

Down the hall to the left was a bathroom, and down a little further was a huge bedroom. On the right, Grey peeked into a family room, complete with a wide screen TV, sleek leather reclining chairs, and video game controls.

The staircase leading to the second floor was to the left of the front door. Grey looked at the steps. She braced herself before she undertook the daunting task of yanking her suitcase behind her as she began the long climb. She felt like she was going to wind up in the clouds. When she finally reached the last step, she sat on her suitcase to rest.

To the left or to the right? She paused. *To the left,* she told herself, remembering the French doors that opened out onto the deck. She couldn't imagine having a room with French doors overlooking the ocean. Michael was not getting that room.

She hurried down the hallway, dragging her suitcase behind her, glancing at the bathroom and a bedroom on the left. The bedroom she wanted would either be at the end of the hallway or on the right side. It seemed like the longest hallway ever. She could hear Michael barreling up the steps behind her.

She saw the closed door at the end of the hallway. *That must be it.* She jerked her suitcase across the last few feet of tile floor, out of breath, but determined to get to the room before Michael. She fumbled with the door handle as Michael reached the last step. He raced down the hallway toward her. She opened the door, leaving her suitcase in the hallway. Grey hurriedly slammed the door closed, locking it just before Michael reached her.

"Let me in. I want to see it!" Michael banged on the door.

Grey leaned her whole body on the door. The cool wood felt good. She ignored Michael and slowly turned around, leaning back on the door. The first thing she noticed was the shine coming from the hardwood floors. The sun's rays came in through the silver French doors to the right and the skylight above, making them appear like glass.

The banging at the door had stopped. Maybe Michael had finally given up and found himself a nice room.

She walked to the doors, turned the silver lock, and pushed them open stepping out onto the deck. A warm, calming breeze surrounded her. She lingered for a moment before turning and walking back into the room, leaving the doors open. There was a queen-sized bed with a white bedspread. Above it was a fan with big paddles that looked like palm leaves. Sparsely furnished, but spacious.

To the left there was a bathroom with a glass shower and sunken tub. What more could a girl ask for? The wall opposite the French doors had a bay window with a window seat. *Good for reading on rainy days.*

Grey heard a thud that caused her to jump and turn around. There, Michael stood on the deck.

"How did you get up here?" she asked.

"I climbed up from the deck downstairs," He walked into the bedroom, looking around nonchalantly. "Nice room."

"I'm taking it, Michael," Grey declared.

Michael walked past her onto the deck. "Relax. I don't want it. I'm taking the one downstairs, so Mom won't hear me when I come in at night." He pulled out his phone again. "Yes! Service. I have to stand right here." He perched precariously on the second railing of the deck.

"You and your stupid phone."

Michael didn't answer Grey. He was staring at his phone.

"What about Mom? What room is she taking?" asked Grey.

"She's taking one of the two at the other end of this hallway. So, she can keep an eye on you." Michael smiled.

Grey rolled her eyes. "Ha, ha."

"Come on, let's bring the rest of the bags in for Mom. Then we can jump in the pool."

They quickly helped their mom and changed into their bathing suits.

Grey carefully stepped into the pool expecting a chill from the cold water, but instead the soothing temperature comforted her. She descended into the pool, allowing the water to rise just above her shoulders. She leaned her head back against the side, closing her eyes. After a few seconds, she heard pounding feet on the pavement. She opened her eyes in time to see Michael, mid-air, doing a cannonball into the deep end. The water splashed all over her, sending the once calm water rushing toward her in waves. Michael broke the surface of the water and shook his head sending beads of water everywhere.

"It's so warm!" He sounded surprised.

"I know!" Grey wiped water from her face.

"Oh, this place just gets better and better!" Michael floated on his back, looking up at the sky.

Grey smiled at her brother and closed her eyes again.

Grey was sitting on her deck trying to get a head start on the required summer reading for school—*Romeo and Juliet* by William Shakespeare. She didn't want to wait until the last minute. The last week had been relatively quiet, and she hadn't left the house except for the occasional dip in the pool or walk on the beach. She liked the solitude she found here, and she liked her little routine. She hadn't had a routine of any kind since her dad died. She felt like she was living in a snow globe that was being constantly shaken.

Grey placed the book on her lap and closed her eyes, grateful for the shade the umbrella gave. The sun was extremely strong and unforgiving. She began to feel herself drifting between that peaceful state of awareness and sleep when a *thump* shook the deck slightly. She jumped, the book flying out of her lap.

Michael stood in front of her with a big grin. "You're coming with me right now."

"Jeez, Michael! What are you doing?"

"Come on!" He pulled her out of the lounge chair by her hand.

"Don't you use doors like normal people?" She struggled to break free from his grasp.

"I'm not normal, and the door is locked."

Grey jerked her hand away. "For a reason Michael!"

"Come on."

"No, I'm busy." Grey searched for her book.

Michael folded his arms, leaning on the railing. "It went over the side."

"What?"

"Your book. It went over the side of the deck. Now it's aaallll the way down there." He pointed over the deck.

"You're kidding!"

"Nope. Guess you'll have to come out of your cave and get it."

Grey walked into her room. "Jerk."

"Is that anyway to talk to your brother who loves you?" Michael followed her.

"Do I bother you? No. So why do you have to bother me?" She unlocked her bedroom door.

"Because that's what brothers do best." He smiled, trailing behind her down the hallway.

She stormed down the steps and out the front door with Michael still right behind her.

"You can't stay in your room for the whole summer."

Grey quickly turned on her heels to face Michael. "Why not?"

"Because it's not healthy."

Grey held onto the banister and ran down the steps. "We've only been here a week, Michael. It's not the whole summer."

Michael rushed after her. "I know, but I also know you, and you'll stay in your room for the whole summer if you don't get out now."

"So what?" She walked to the side of the house looking for the book.

"So what?" Michael parroted, almost knocking Grey over as he quickly pushed past her and picked up the book. "There's a whole key to explore," he continued.

Grey reached for the book. "Give it to me."

"No." He held it over his head.

Grey clenched her teeth. "Michael!"

Michael drew his arm back and threw it up on the deck. "There. Go get it."

Grey scoffed. She ran to the front of the house, up the steps, and into the house. She continued to her bedroom and ran onto the deck, out of breath. There she saw Michael sitting on the railing of the deck, thumbing through her book.

"Michael, give it to me!"

"What took you so long?" Michael closed the book and smiled before dangling it over the side of the deck.

Grey held onto the deck trying to catch her breath. "Michael, no."

"No?"

"Michael!" Grey yelled, frustrated.

"What?" he playfully asked, pretending to fumble and then catch it safely in his hands.

"No, please!" she begged.

Michael laughed.

"It's not funny!"

"It kind of is."

"Michael, give it to me!" she demanded, half laughing.

"Only if you come for a ride with me."

"Why?" she whined, still trying to catch her breath.

"Because you're my sister." He let the book slip a little from his fingers.

"No!"

"I could do this all day."

"Fine!" she said, stomping her foot.

"You'll come with me?"

"Yes." She glared at him.

Michael stepped back from the railing. "Okay, because I just want to be sure."

The last thing Grey wanted to do was go for a ride with her brother, but she didn't want to play this game with him any longer.

Grey tried to grab the book one last time, but Michael quickly put it behind his back, ducking around her as he ran into her room. Grey took a deep breath and followed Michael, dragging her feet.

Chapter Four

"Wait up!" Grey yelled out to Michael who pedaled down the driveway. He turned right, disappearing with her copy of *Romeo and Juliet* tucked in the back waistband of his shorts. Grey finally caught up with her brother. They rode, going from the bike lane to the occasional sidewalk, dodging the Spanish moss and overgrown vines that hung from the trees, passing one house more interesting than the last. Rarely were there any cars in the driveways. They seemed abandoned, except for the impeccable landscaping that was meant to look intentionally overgrown.

How nice just coasting along down the empty road with her brother. She was enjoying the breeze on her face, the way it blew her hair back. There was freedom in riding the bike. So, maybe Michael was right. Perhaps she was missing out on things by not getting out, but she wasn't about to let Michael know that.

Michael slowed down so he could ride next to Grey.

"Now, is this so bad?" he teased.

"It's terrible," she said, looking straight ahead before

looking at him and smiling.

Michael just shook his head.

"Why do you have to be so stubborn?"

"I'm not stubborn."

They both laughed.

They pedaled quietly for a while, turning down side streets and admiring the beautiful landscape of the key.

"Grey, Mom is going to ask you to come to a drum circle with us tonight and I think you should come."

Grey stiffened. *Here it comes.*

She dreaded doing things with Mom and Michael. For Grey, it was a glaring reminder that one person was missing. The feelings that were brought to the surface were unbearable to endure. She tried to push them away, keeping them bottled up deep down. She didn't know how to deal with any of it.

Grey didn't have any reaction when Dad died. No tears. No yelling. Nothing. It didn't mean that she didn't love Dad; she did. He was her hero. She remembered everything he did for her growing up. It's funny how that happens when someone dies. You remember everything they ever did for you and said to you. When she was little, she would ask him to pick her up so she could see on top of the refrigerator. She thought he was so tall. She remembered all the games they would play, their Sunday walks to get the newspaper, and all the times he encouraged her to do the things she wanted to do but thought she couldn't. He also told her she was just as good as the other girls. Mom worried about her, but she wished she would just leave her alone.

"Look, she's sacrificing a lot for us, and she doesn't ask

much," Michael reminded.

This was true, but Grey didn't know how to answer. She had had her guard up since Dad got sick years ago that she honestly had forgotten how to be any other way. She felt like she didn't have a say in anything he was going through. She couldn't help him, so being stubborn was how she dealt with this, whether she was right or wrong. It was her way of being able to hold onto what little control she had left, a form of protection. Her way of being strong for Dad and her family. At least, that's what she thought.

"I know," she whispered.

"So, think about it. Okay?"

She nodded.

"Come on, I'll race you to the end of the key!"

Grey looked at Michael, uninterested.

Michael pedaled ahead of Grey. "I heard there are snakes here."

With that, Grey pedaled hard and fast to catch up with her brother and passed him. She hated snakes!

Down the road she saw a sign that read Tortoise Beach. She took the right down the black paved road continuing to pedal hard. The road veered left leading to a small beach. Michael followed, and together they raced the length of the narrow parking lot to the very end of the key. Grey reached the end first, skidding as she hit the brakes. She straddled her bike looking out over the ocean, then closed her eyes, breathing in the salt air.

"So, you're pretty fast when you wanna be," Michael called out, a little out of breath, coming to a screeching halt next to her.

"I can hold my own," Grey said, smiling.

"Did you see that dirt path back there?"

"No. I didn't."

"Come on, let's go take a look," he said as he threw her copy of *Romeo and Juliet* into her silver metal bike basket.

"Okay."

Michael took off, leaving Grey to catch up again. He tore down the parking lot, turning up sand that had gathered on the black pavement. *Thanks Michael.* She hung back a little so she wouldn't get the sand in her face.

Once out onto the road, Grey pedaled faster to catch up with her brother. To the left and right she swerved, ducking to avoid the hanging vines that hung from the trees. She switched to a higher gear to catch up with Michael. The muscles in her legs burned. She switched gears again, but something wasn't right. The gears made a clicking noise and weren't engaging. She looked down to see what was going on, shifting gears again. Finally, the clicking noise stopped. She looked back up, *smack!* Hanging vines hit Grey in the face, causing her to almost lose control of the bike. She steadied the handlebars to recover.

Grey picked the small leaves and twigs out of her hair as she rode. One of the twigs wriggled, and she screamed, flicking away whatever was in her hand. Her bike wobbled from side to side. Trying to gain control, she had a split second to decide: pavement or shrubbery, pavement, or shrubbery?! She turned the handlebars to the left; into the shrubbery she fell.

Michael looked back over his shoulder. "Grey!" His tires

squealed as he turned around, pedaling to his sister. "Are you alright?" Michael asked when he made it back to her.

Grey sat up. "What was that?"

"What was what?" Michael helped her up out of the shrubbery.

"It was in my hair. It was moving. I threw it over there!" She shuddered.

Grey watched Michael walk into the middle of the road. He inspected the area, finally bending down, and picked up something.

He strolled back toward Grey with his hand behind his back. She saw the smirk on his face as she brushed herself off, checking for cuts and scrapes.

"This?" He held out what appeared to be a twig.

"What is it?" It was moving. A snake! Grey screamed.

Michael laughed. "It's only a snake."

"Get it away from me!" Grey said, quickly stepping back.

"It's kind of cute. Don't you think?" He held it up to his face.

"Michael! Stop it!" Grey screamed.

"Grey, it can't hurt you."

"Michael!" she screeched, stamping her foot.

Michael smiled shaking his head. He gently tossed it into the shrubbery before picking up her bike. "Are you sure you're okay?"

"Yeah, I'm fine. I hate snakes!" She shuddered, picking up her copy of *Romeo and Juliet* off the ground and placing it in her basket.

"Come on, let's go." Michael jumped onto his bike.

Grey got on her bike, cautiously looking up at the trees.

"Wait up Michael!" Grey yelled, pedaling fast to catch up with him.

Michael didn't slow down. He turned down the narrow dirt path into the woods. Grey was surprised that Michael had seen the path because it really didn't look like a path at all. It was barely wide enough for one bike. They rode past tall old palm trees and through the overgrown, dense bushes. Michael rode hard and fast. She was now quite a distance behind him. She pedaled faster and faster, but the dirt path was harder to ride on than the smooth pavement of the road.

So much for Michael protecting me from the snakes.

Michael stopped. She rode up behind him. He was staring ahead, mesmerized. She followed his gaze. There in the middle of the woods, among the overgrown, twisted foliage and trees, was a beautiful clearing encircled by white-skinned trees that stretched for the sky. Their branches and leaves intertwined, forming a canopy above like a perfectly enclosed circle. Their trunks were so wide you could hide behind them.

They must be really old. If she tried to wrap her arms around one of the trees, they wouldn't go halfway around. Within the circle was the purest greenest grass. There weren't any leaves or brush on the grass either, which was odd. It looked perfectly manicured. *Who would do this all the way out here?*

They stood there for a few moments straddling their bikes until they finally looked at each other.

"What is it?" Grey whispered.

"I don't know," Michael whispered back.

The key was usually quiet, but there was an unusual quiet

here that made Grey and Michael afraid to speak.

"Come on," Grey said softly, slowly getting off her bike and lowering it to the ground.

"What are you doing?"

Grey ignored her brother.

Michael stood there for a moment before getting off his bike, cautiously following her.

As they entered the clearing, the air itself seemed to be filled with light. Light you could breathe in. It was simple yet beautiful. Grey immediately noticed that she felt different, but what was it?

"Do you feel that?" Michael quietly asked.

Grey nodded, still afraid to speak. After a moment, Grey turned to her brother and calmly asked, "You feel it too?"

"I do," he replied.

"It's a . . ." Grey tried to search for the right word, "peacefulness, a lightness."

Wow. She hadn't felt this in years. Calm, warm, no worries. She was truly, purely happy. Total ecstasy. *How odd. Odd but wonderful!*

The leaves rustled above them breaking the silence. Grey and Michael quickly looked up, then slowly at each other. Stillness. A sound so simple, so normal for where they were, made their hearts race. There was a *swoosh* overhead. A soft breeze passed them. Stillness again. They froze, afraid to look up.

A thud behind them. They jumped. Grey grabbed Michael's hand. They slowly turned around.

A black leather-bound book with yellowed, tattered paper

peeking out around the worn edges, lay on the soft green grass. The air seemed to swirl around the book, and one sun-ray allowed through the dense canopy of trees overhead, gently illuminated it. Grey and Michael looked up only to see the tree branches covering them in silence. Nothing moved.

Grey's adrenaline coursed through her body. *What was it? Where did it come from?* It wasn't there a few seconds ago. She looked at Michael, who was frozen. His grip tightened on her hand. He widened his eyes, shaking his head slightly from side to side. He was trying to tell her not to go near it.

She tried to pry her brother's hand away from hers, but he wouldn't let her. She quickly pulled her hand away from his, carefully taking a step closer to the book. It was so quiet she could hear the grass bend under her feet, rippling through her body. She stopped. After a moment, she took another step, slowly looking back at her brother. He stared at her. She curiously, but cautiously, knelt in front of the book. There was something engraved in the leather, but she couldn't make it out because it was so old and worn. All she could hear was her heart pounding in her chest and she slowly reached down, her hand trembling. It lingered there for what seemed like an eternity. Why was she scared? The book looked so ancient, like something from another time . . . another world.

She took a deep breath and lightly touched the book. A moment went by. Nothing. Quiet. Her breath quickened. She slowly reached out to touch it again. Her finger was just about to graze the book, when a piercing cry of rage rang out. Grey and Michael quickly covered their ears. The winds forcefully began to swirl around them. The thick old tree limbs bent, twisting angrily. Leaves violently torn from their branches, swirling around them like a cyclone. Michael ran to his sister, grabbing her as they were forced to the ground by the powerful winds. They huddled together, holding onto each other, terrified. The storm was so loud they couldn't hear their own screams. The strong winds lifted Michael away from Grey, throwing him down on the ground. A violent, ice-cold gust rushed past them with a vicious growl, pushing them further into the earth.

Silence . . . it came as quickly as it went.

Grey was afraid to move, unsure if Michael was okay.

Is it over? What was it? Grey kept her eyes shut tight, afraid to look, her body frozen. She felt something on her outstretched leg and pulled it quickly to her body. *Oh no! What is it?*

She heard a whisper. "Grey . . ."

She was confused. Was it real?

"Grey . . ." Again, she heard it. Her head spun. She was terrified.

Oh, please make it go away.

"Grey . . . Grey, are you alright?"

She realized it was Michael. Slowly she lifted her head, keeping it close to the earth. She turned slightly.

Michael lay on the ground where the wind had thrown him, his hair disheveled, his clothes torn. "What the hell was that?" Michael whispered.

"I don't know," Grey said, still afraid to move. *Was it going to come back?*

Michael stood cautiously. "Come on."

Grey, still in the same position on the ground, pushed herself up. She surveyed the area. Just as it was when they first got there. Calm. Nothing out of place, as if nothing had happened.

Michael's outstretched hand trembled as he helped his sister up. "Let's get out of here."

Still confused, she took his hand. His face was ashen. She heard a light patter and grabbed his arm. "What's that?"

Michael listened for a moment and looked up. "Rain," he said, breathing a sigh of relief.

Grey looked up. She saw the leaves and palms lightly vibrating from the falling rain.

"Let's go!" Michael ran toward the bikes.

Grey quickly followed, then stopped and turned around. *The book?* She wondered, confused.

Michael jumped on his bike.

Grey looked where the book was. Nothing. It was gone.

It was there. She did touch it. She felt it.

A loud crack of thunder shook the ground, quickly snapping her out of her thoughts.

"Grey, come on! It's going to pour!"

She turned toward Michael, running to her bike. She swung her leg over the seat, latching the top of her foot on the pedal to bring it back around and up so she could quickly push off, but something stopped her.

It was real, wasn't it? She had to turn around one more time!

There was nothing there but the beautiful, white-skinned trees and the perfect grass.

Michael was pedaling down the path, moving farther

away from her. She was getting cold from the chilly air that was moving in with the rain. She turned to catch up with Michael, and stopped again. Something caught her eye. What was it? She tried to make it out far off in the clearing next to one of the trees. Whatever it was, it wasn't there before.

Could it be? She squinted her eyes.

It was! A male figure with straight, dark hair that grazed his shoulders and piercing blue eyes. Though far away, she could see his eyes, they were so blue.

He stared right at her. He didn't move. A cold chill ran through her. She could feel her heart pounding through her whole body.

"Grey!" Michael screamed for her in the distance.

She abruptly turned to pedal, frightened. She pedaled with all she had in her to catch up with him. The wet brush that jutted out into the small path hit Grey, stinging and scratching her body. The rain came down heavier making the leaf-covered path slick. She was reminded of the spill she took earlier. Damn snakes!

She could see the road ahead and Michael waiting for her.

"Come on!" Michael tried to steady himself against the powerful wind as he started on his bike again.

She pedaled out onto the road. The inky black sky loomed above, covered by the protecting trees. It was like another world back there.

The rain was falling hard now. So hard, in fact, that if she screamed, Michael wouldn't have heard her. The road ahead was difficult to see, and the rain's little needles pricked her skin as it hit her body. Lightening zigzagged above her, followed by earth shattering thunder. Grey had never seen anything like this before. She pedaled against the wind, her body stiff from the cold air that blew in with the storm. It was hard to see Michael through the rain that streamed into her eyes.

She almost passed the driveway but quickly turned the handlebars with a jerk, barely making it.

"Grey, hurry up!" Michael yelled as she got closer. He was in the garage, totally soaked, like he had just gone swimming. Grey raced in, using the hand brakes only when she was under the cover of the garage, causing the tires to leave skid marks on the white floor.

They ran up the steps, bursting into the house. Mom came down the steps as they stood in the hallway trying to catch their breath.

"What happened to you two?" Mom's voice sounded concerned.

"We went for a bike ride, and it started to rain," Michael bent over with his hands on his knees, breathing heavily.

"Your clothes!" Mom looked exasperated.

Grey looked down. Her clothes were torn. She didn't feel like getting into this with Mom right now. She didn't even know what really happened back there.

"It's, it's fr-fr-freezing." Grey began to shiver.

"Well, go change before you get sick," Mom instructed.

Grey ran past Mom to her room. The only thing she could think about was how cold she was. *Into the shower, a nice hot shower.* Quickly, she walked into the marble bathroom, reaching into the glass shower stall, and turned on the hot water full force. She made sure the water didn't touch her because it would be cold at first. The thought of it made her shiver even more. She closed the bathroom door, sat on the edge of the tub, and thought about what had happened.

"How could it be?" She did see the book. She touched it. The male figure! Surely, she saw him. Right? she asked herself as the bathroom filled with steam.

Chapter Five

The dinner table was set. Michael and Mom were already seated when Grey walked into the kitchen.

"What took you so long?" Mom asked. "Dinner is getting cold."

"I took a shower. I was freezing." Grey sat down, the sun was shining. "It stopped raining?" she asked, a little surprised.

Mom looked outside. "Yes. Apparently, it downpours here, and then the sun comes out."

"Not like back home where if it rains, it rains all day," Michael said, stuffing a forkful of food into his mouth.

Grey ate slowly, still thinking about what had happened earlier. She looked at Michael. Nothing. He was eating without a care in the world. It figured. Michael had a way of never letting anything bother him. He would just shrug his shoulders and let it roll off his back. The only time she had really seen him upset was when Dad died. Oh, and the time his turtle died when they were seven. Dad and a turtle. *Go figure.*

"Grey, aren't you hungry?" Mom pointed toward Grey's plate with her fork.

"I guess I'm not," she said, pushing her food around on her plate.

"Are you okay?"

"I'm fine, Mom. I think I'm just tired." Grey looked at Michael sitting across from her. He put a bite in his mouth and gave her a quick smile. *How could he smile?*

He went back to eating. She stared at him. Nothing could ruin his appetite. It was amazing.

"I thought we could go for a walk on the beach after dinner," said Mom.

"That sounds good to me," Michael said.

They both looked at Grey, lost in thought. No reply.

"Grey?" Mom asked.

"What?"

"Would you like to go for a walk on the beach?"

Grey stiffened. "Ummm . . ."

"Come on. They have this drum circle down on White Beach at sunset. It'll be fun," Mom said, getting up from the table and refilling her glass of water.

"What's that?" asked Michael.

"I'm not really sure, but the owners mentioned it to me. They said that people gather there every Sunday at sunset, and they bring their drums and play music."

"You mean there are people that actually live here?" Michael's voice dripped with sarcasm.

"Yes, there are people that actually live here, Michael. You're just used to back home where it's so busy all the time," Mom said as she threw a dish towel at him.

"Well, I'm up for it. Grey'll come too," he said, putting

the last bite of food in his mouth.

Grey shot him a look. He gave her the same look back, and then smiled at her.

"Good," Mom said.

Michael picked up his plate and put it in the dishwasher. "Are you done, Mom?"

"Yes, I'm done."

He took her plate and quickly grabbed Grey's plate, full of food, right out from under her.

"Hey, I'm not finished!"

"Yes, you are," Michael put the dishes in the dishwasher. He grabbed Mom and Grey by the hands, pulling them out the sliding glass doors onto the deck. "Let's go." He ran down the steps onto the beach. Mom and Grey slowly trailed behind.

They walked down to the water and continued along the shoreline, watching the tiny waves gently crashing on the beach. The warm water tickled their feet as it glided along the wet sand. The sun hung above the horizon, and any traces of rain that had fallen earlier were gone. The powdery sand was the whitest Grey had ever seen. She never felt ocean water so warm. It was like bathwater. She looked out over the horizon. She loved the ocean. There was something calming about it though it was so big and powerful.

"So, where did you two go today?"

Grey stiffened.

"We just rode to the end of the key. Did a little exploring," said Michael.

"Is it nice?" Mom asked.

"Yeah."

"Did you see anything interesting?" she asked.

Grey looked straight ahead. Her heart beat faster.

"Yes, as a matter of fact, we did," he said, smiling.

Grey's eyes almost popped out of her head.

"A snake," he said, laughing.

Mom stopped in her tracks. "A what?!"

"A snake fell from a tree and landed on Grey." He laughed harder.

A wave of relief came over Grey. She had no idea what was going to come out of his mouth.

"It really wasn't funny," she protested.

"And then she fell into the bushes." He was laughing so hard now he had to stop walking. "She had twigs and leaves in her hair. It was hysterical!"

"Is that how you got the scrape on your leg?" Mom sounded concerned.

Grey looked down to see a long scrape on her left leg. "Oh, look at that," she said. Grey hadn't noticed it until now. Odd she hadn't felt it either.

"Be careful," Mom shuddered. "I hate snakes."

"Me too," said Grey.

"Obviously." Michael snorted.

Grey lightly nudged her brother's arm.

"You should come next time, Mom."

"Not if there are snakes, Michael!"

"I'll protect you, Mom." He put his arm around her.

They laughed.

"Can you hear the drums?" Mom asked, reaching out for Grey's hand. Off in the distance, the pulse of the drums reverberated, and people gathered on the beach.

"Hmm mmm," Grey said, letting her hand linger in Mom's before slowly pulling away.

"It looks like it's going to be cool. Come on, Grey, it's something different!" Michael purposely bumped into her, causing her to stumble. They all laughed.

White Beach was the public beach on Sleepy Key. People gathered at sunset sitting in chairs, on blankets, or in the sand, and listened as people played their drums and an occasional guitar. It was basically a big jam session.

People were milling around the already created circle in which a roaring bonfire was the centerpiece. Grey, Michael, and Mom walked around trying to find the best spot to stand and take it all in. They had never experienced anything like this back home. There were all different kinds of people; from hippies, who looked like they hadn't showered in weeks, to young couples, rockers, teenagers, and adults, to retired folks who just came to enjoy the music and the atmosphere.

They found a small opening in the drum circle closest to the water. They stood and watched as one person started a beat on their drum. Then, someone joined in, and someone else, and another person until the air was filled with a beautiful rhythm.

Grey scanned the crowd, entertained by all the different people. The children, most of them covered in sand, ran around chasing each other, pretending to play their colorful, plastic instruments. The parents seemed so carefree, not worrying about where they were or what they were doing. The hippies with their long dreadlocks that were dyed different colors, dressed in tie-dye clothes, danced with abandon. Retired people reclined in their beach chairs with coffee mugs and the occasional flask, tapping their feet in the sand. Teenagers stood around the outside of the drum circle, in groups, talking somewhat away from the crowd.

Grey had never seen a bonfire before. She watched the flames as they licked the air and liked the way some of the smaller logs would fall into the sand sending sparks into the air. The crackling they made reminded her of a whip being snapped. She was mesmerized by the experience, swaying to the beat of the drums. She hadn't realized it was nightfall until the bonfire flames cast shadows, dancing on everyone's faces. Everyone seemed to be having a good time. It was so simple, yet so perfect.

Grey stood a few feet from Mom. She found herself smiling as she watched her lightly sway to the beat of the music. Her smile soon faded as she noticed for the first time that Mom had a few lines on her face. The shadows from the flames crossed over, making the lines appear deeper, giving Grey a glimpse into what Mom would look like when she got older. Grey had always thought her mom was beautiful, and now it made her sad. Not because they made her any less beautiful, but because for the first time, she realized time was taking her away little by little. She was very aware of time lately. She wanted to get close to Mom, but something held her back, and she wasn't quite sure what it was. The only thing she knew was she didn't feel this way until Dad died.

"So, what do you think?" Michael asked. "Pretty cool, huh?"

"Yeah."

"See, it's not so bad doing things with your family, now is it?"

"No," she said reluctantly, playfully pushing her brother.

"Let's walk around," Michael said.

"Okay," Grey replied, still looking at Mom.

"Mom, we'll be right back," said Michael.

"Okay, have fun."

Grey and Michael walked around the perimeter of the circle, leaving Mom alone.

There must have been at least two hundred people there. A group of teenagers stood together down by the ocean. There was something different about them. The way they dressed, the way they stood, the way they moved, the way they looked. Flawless white skin that illuminated in the night. Some with hair so dark it stood out against the black sky. Others with hair so light it was almost blinding. Enthralled, Grey walked slower, unaware she was losing her brother who walked ahead. Grey scanned over them, one more beautiful than the next, until she got to the last one . . . she froze. She felt as if her feet had become sucked into the sand. She told herself to move but nothing happened. Her heart raced. Her eyes were fixed on . . . someone.

Could it be? Her heart raced even faster. She no longer heard the beating of the drums. *Oh my God!* It was the boy she had seen earlier that day in the woods, and he was staring right at her! It was like he was calling to her. He looked at her the same way he did earlier in the woods. Standing, not moving, while the others he was with talked among themselves, hanging out the way teenagers did.

Michael! Where was Michael? She scanned the crowd, but he had disappeared.

She turned to the group of teenagers again. The boy from the woods was standing right in front of her. He stared at her for a moment.

"Hi," he said in a voice lower than she had expected.

Grey didn't reply. All she could think about was how fast her heart was beating. He continued to stare at her. His straight, shoulder-length hair fell forward as he lowered his head a little, never taking his eyes off her.

"I'm Zale," he said.

He was taller than Grey. She was transfixed by his flawless skin and full lips. He seemed to be a little older than her by the way he carried himself with such confidence. She also felt a worldliness from him.

"Hi." She diverted her eyes away from his, digging her toes in the sand. *Where was Michael?!* she screamed in her head.

"You are beautiful," he said, never taking his eyes off her.

No one had ever called Grey beautiful before, except her parents, but they didn't count. Light perspiration dampened her face, and her cheeks warmed. Her heart thudded in her ears. Could he hear it? Why did this always happen when she talked to boys?

Turn away from the flames and he won't be able to see. When she looked up again, Zale was gazing past her shoulder. She turned. What was so interesting? A group of teenagers, similar to the group Zale was with, stood several yards behind her. One of the girls had red ribbons for laces in her combat boots.

They stared at him.

Grey wondered if he knew them.

"I don't really know them," said Zale.

"What?" Grey asked, confused.

"You looked like you were wondering if I knew them," Zale replied.

"Oh, I—"

"There you are, Grey."

Grey spun around, relieved. "Michael!"

"I was looking for you," Michael said, not acknowledging Zale.

"Ah. Grey," Zale said, "that is your name."

Grey grabbed Michael's hand as Michael noticed Zale standing behind her.

"Oh hey, I'm Michael." Michael extended his hand, but Zale just smiled and kept his hands at his side.

"I'm Zale. I was just telling your sister how beautiful she is." Zale put his hands behind his back.

Michael let his extended hand slowly fall to his side, his smile fading.

"Yeah, I tell her that all the time, but she doesn't listen to me."

Grey dug her nails into Michael's hand.

"Ow!" Michael exclaimed. "Well, we've gotta go. See you around," Michael said, seemingly unimpressed with Zale. He walked away, pulling Grey with him lightly.

"I hope so. We're here every Sunday," Zale said, staring

at Grey.

She smiled at him. She was afraid to look at him, but, at the same time, she wanted to. As Grey and her brother walked away, she turned around again. This time Zale was surrounded by his friends. *How did they get to him so quickly?* They were watching them walk back to the drum circle. The next time Grey had the courage to turn around . . . they were gone.

"Who was that?" Michael asked.

"I don't know," she said, still holding her brother's hand.

"Well, he sure liked you."

There was no reply from Grey. Her head was swimming with questions. She was confused and excited at the same time. *What was he doing here? Why was he in the woods? Did he have anything to do with the book?*

"And why are you holding my hand?"

"Shut up," she said, and pulled away.

Chapter Six

Grey stopped for a moment and looked at herself in the bathroom mirror as she brushed her teeth. She was so frustrated that Michael hadn't talked to her about what happened earlier in the day. He had to think it was strange. How could he not want to talk about it? Well, if he wasn't going to bring it up, she would. She rinsed her mouth and walked out of the bathroom.

Grey walked into Michael's room and found him lying in bed, reading a book. The lamp on the nightstand illuminated a bright white light.

"I need to talk to you."

"Don't you even knock?"

Grey plopped down on the edge of Michael's bed.

"No, not now," she said, looking directly at him. "Are we ever going to talk about what happened today?"

"What's there to talk about?" he said, shrugging his shoulders.

"You don't know?"

Michael just looked at Grey.

"That guy, Zale. I saw him in the woods today."

"What?" Michael asked, skeptically.

"Yeah. After you took off and left me there all by myself, I turned around, and I saw him leaning against a tree."

"I think you need some sleep," he said, going back to his reading.

"I saw him, Michael."

"Well, I don't know what he would be doing leaning against a tree in the middle of the woods in the rain."

"Me, neither."

"Maybe you should've asked him."

"And how did he know we were brother and sister?" she said, ignoring Michael's sarcasm.

"What are you talking about?" he said, getting a little annoyed.

"When you came over, he said, 'I was talking to your sister.'"

"Umm, no, he said, 'I was just telling your sister how beeeeuuutiiful she is.'" Michael beamed.

"Stop it, Michael," Grey said, as her face flushed. "I need you to be serious."

"How did he know we were brother and sister?"

"I don't know, maybe he just figured we were."

"How?"

"I don't know. We're twins. Look, you're reading too much into this."

"No, I'm not," she said. "We don't even look alike." Grey looked at Michael who just laid there. "Maybe he had something to do with the book."

Michael looked away. "I don't know, Grey."

"That's it? You don't know?"

"I don't know," he replied flatly.

"You *saw* the book."

"I don't want to talk about it."

"How can you not want to talk about it? Aren't you curious? What was it? What happened?"

"Some things you just can't explain."

Grey leaned closer to her brother. "You're not even curious?" she asked.

"I knew this was coming." He closed his book, propping himself up against the dark brown headboard.

Grey sighed heavily. "Are you going to tell me you didn't see the book?"

"I'm tired, and I want to go to bed," said Michael.

"You know you saw it."

Michael looked away.

Grey watched him for a moment waiting for a response.

"I touched it!" she said excitedly, raising her voice.

"Shhhh! You'll wake Mom."

"You know you saw it," Grey said, lowering her voice to a loud whisper. "And then the swirling, twirling wind . . . what was that all about?"

"It was just the storm coming in."

"It was not, and you know it," she said in a hushed voice. "What's wrong with you? Why don't you want to talk about it?"

Michael closed his book and put it on the nightstand. He turned back to Grey and stared at her for a moment. "Grey, whatever went on out there today, it scared the hell out of me," he said, looking down at his hands. "And you know things don't usually scare me. I didn't want you to touch that book. I was frozen and couldn't get to you to pull you away. I didn't . . ." Michael sighed. "I couldn't protect you. There was just something terrifying about it . . . The last time I felt that way was when Dad died. When I couldn't protect him. Okay? So, did I see the book? Yes, I saw it," he said, reluctantly. "Do I want to know what it was or why it happened? No. I just want to enjoy our time here."

There was silence for a moment. Grey looked at her brother. He was right. He was never afraid. It was weird having the tables turned.

"You know, when we get home, I have to take his place. I need to fill his shoes and they're some pretty big shoes to fill. I worry about that, and I feel guilty because I know I can't do it. I can't do what he did, but I have to help Mom financially. I should probably be working now. I'm sure Mom's worried about money."

Grey was silent as she rolled a loose thread on the bedspread between her fingers. She hadn't really thought about all of that. "Okay, Michael, but like you said, can't we just enjoy our time here and not think about it until we get home?"

"Going to look for something in the middle of the woods that terrified me is not enjoyable," he said, fidgeting with the sheets.

"Michael . . . I really want to know what it was," she said, slowly.

"Why? Why is it so important?"

"I don't know. It's like it's calling me."

Michael stared at his sister blankly.

"Will you *please* go back with me tomorrow?" she asked nicely.

"No," he said flatly.

"Please, Michael," she begged, tucking her legs underneath her.

"No."

"I'll do anything for you," she said. "I'll do your chores for the rest of the summer."

"I don't want you to do anything for me, and I like doing my chores."

"Michael!"

"Shhhh!" Michael said, as he put a finger up to his lips. "No, we have to help Mom around here."

"Oh yeah, like that's going to take all day." She clasped her hands in front of her. "Come on Michael, come with me. Please don't make me go by myself."

Michael shot her a look.

He would never let her go by herself. If anything ever happened to her, she knew he would never forgive himself. Michael always protected her.

Michael thought for a moment. "Fine," he said, reluctantly.

"Oh, thank you, Michael," she said, hugging him.

"Good night," he said, lightly pushing her away.

"Good night, Michael," She ran out of his room before he could change his mind.

Quickly Grey went up the steps and down the hallway. Careful not to wake Mom, she passed by her bedroom. Grey double-checked the French doors in her room and looked out into the night. She always made sure all the doors were locked in the house. That was something Dad always did too. Mom and Michael called them The Lockkeepers.

The bright white moon reflected its light on the water. Afraid to really look around for fear of what, or whom, she might see, Grey pulled the curtains shut, quickly jumping into bed. She pulled the sheet over her head, allowing her face to peek out.

As she laid there, she went over the events of the day in her head. There was no way it wasn't real. Over and over again, she replayed things until she finally fell asleep.

The moon shone through the skylight and onto Grey's face as she slept peacefully. Suddenly, a long shadow was cast onto her from the skylight. Zale peered through the skylight watching Grey.

Chapter Seven

Grey, filled with anticipation, sat straight up on her bike as she pedaled down the tree-lined road with Michael. The light breeze blew through the leaves on the trees above, casting ever-changing shadows on the road.

Would she see Zale again?

Grey surprised Mom by volunteering to go to the store for her this morning. She figured this would give her the opportunity to go back to the spot in the woods while doing something for Mom at the same time.

See, I am trying. She smiled.

As they got closer to the trail, Grey slowed down a little bit.

Michael rode up alongside her. "What's the matter?' he asked, dryly.

"Nothing. Why?"

"Well, you were pedaling like there was a fire behind you, and now you're creeping along like a snail. You're not getting scared, are you?"

"No," she hesitated.

They came to the trail that led to the opening. They

both stopped.

"Well?" said Michael.

"What?"

"Aren't you going to go?"

She pretended to look around, buying herself more time. "Yeah." She wasn't going to let him know that she was a little scared. Okay, maybe more than a little scared. *It was so peaceful. How could anything bad be here?*

"Come on," Michael said, giving in, turning down the trail first.

They stood, straddling their bikes on the edge of the clearing. They were both a little hesitant to give up their bikes.

It was just as she had remembered it. Quiet, peaceful . . . like it didn't belong here.

"Now what?" asked Michael in a soft voice.

"I don't know," Grey replied in almost a whisper.

She got off her bike after a moment, leaning it on a tree. The only sound were the leaves crunching under her feet.

Tentatively she walked to the opening, waving to her brother to follow without turning around. Michael leaned his bike against the nearest tree, trailing after Grey. Her eyes followed the massive trees up to the sky. She walked to the tree where she saw Zale and touched it. She ran her hands over it wondering how long it had been there. It was remarkably smooth, like glass.

She stood in the middle of the opening and looked up. Nothing. Tree branches and leaves gracefully swayed in the breeze. She looked over at Michael who was slowly checking around, obviously just as curious as her, but not wanting to admit it.

They moved through the clearing to see what was on the other side and found it led to the beach. There was no one as far as they could see. A beautiful sunny day, and no one anywhere.

"There's nothing here, Grey. Let's go."

"Alright," Grey sighed, a little disappointed.

They went back to the opening and got on their bikes.

"Michael, you know it happened."

"Yeah, but I don't know," he said, shaking his head. "Maybe it was some freak thing."

"No, there has to be an explanation for it."

They both looked back at the opening before pedaling away.

The opening was quiet. At the far end closest to the ocean stood Zale and his friends.

"So, what now?" asked the tall one leaning against the tree, not bothering to look up from the book she was reading.

"I have an idea Minna. A plan, if you will," replied Zale, a slick smile coming across his face.

"Let's have some fun with this. Afterall, it's so boring here lately," he continued, leaning against one of the white-skinned trees, watching Grey and Michael disappear down the path.

"She touched it," said Newel, disgustedly, sitting in the grass leaning back on her hands, her long dark hair blowing gently in the light breeze.

". . . and I had to get it," said Minna, annoyed, looking

up from her book for a brief moment. "They probably would have let her take it."

"And do you think I was not there and did not see this?" Zale flatly asked, his eyes fixed on the trail in which Grey rode down.

"They dropped the book and handed her right to us," Lars smiled, wickedly.

"Yes, they did. They must be beside themselves," Zale chuckled.

Newel and Lars smiled in agreement.

"I don't like the fact that she could see the Crest. This is our place. Humans aren't able to see it," Minna complained, nonchalantly, her face still buried in the book.

"They both saw it," Lars pointed out.

"Yes, why them?" asked Newel.

"They are twins, so they are connected, but we will find out," Zale assured.

"Why did you have to show yourself to her?" Minna asked, continuing to read the book.

"Because now, I have claimed her . . . and it will be fun," he said, satisfied with himself.

Chapter Eight

Grey frantically looked through her room. *Where was it?* She panicked. It had to be here somewhere. She opened the French doors and walked out onto the deck. The sun was shining brightly, high in the sky. Grey shielded her eyes from it so she could see. She walked over to the table. The sick feeling she had in the pit of her stomach grew. *Where is it?*

She walked into her room and continued down the hallway, running down the steps into the living room. She looked around, picking up her pace as she went through to the kitchen.

Think. Think. When did you see it last? She tried to calm herself. The bike!

She hurried out the door, down the front steps, and lifted the garage door open. She ran over to the bike and looked in the basket. Empty. Grey put her hands to her head. It was gone. Her *Romeo and Juliet* book—gone.

"Okay, when was the last time you saw it. Retrace your steps," she said aloud as her stomach began to churn. She tried to remember, but images were scrambling in her head.

She took a deep breath. *Michael was teasing me about the book. Okay.* They had gone for a ride, and he gave it to her at the end of the key. She paced in the garage. *Gear trouble, I fell, Snake! Eeewww snake!* She shuddered. *That damn snake. Wait, focus.* She had picked up the book and put it in the basket. Grey looked over at the basket again. *Empty. Through the woods . . . oh no! The clearing! The rain!* She must've lost her book on the way home in the storm. She and Michael had gone back to the clearing, and she didn't see anything. Of course, she wasn't looking for it, but she would have seen it, wouldn't she have?

Michael poked his head in the garage.

"Are you ready?"

Grey continued searching.

". . . Um, yes. I'm ready. I'll meet you out back."

"Okay," Michael said before leaving.

Grey looked around one last time before she walked to the garage door, closed it, and ran up the steps into the house.

"Okay, Mom, we'll see you later!" Grey said, running out the sliding doors to the kitchen.

Mom walked onto the deck. "I don't like that we can't reach each other by phone with this no service thing. Don't be too late."

"We won't," said Grey.

Michael was waiting on the beach for Grey.

Grey was a little excited to see if Zale would be at the bonfire, but she couldn't let Michael know. He would never let her hear the end of it.

Grey could feel Michael looking at her as they walked

down the beach. *What was he doing?*

He just kept staring like he was trying to figure out what was different about her. She pretended not to notice until she couldn't take it anymore.

"What?"

"What do you have on your eyes?" Michael looked closely at her.

"Nothing," she said, turning her head slightly away from him as she picked up the pace.

"Look at me," he said, running ahead and walking backward in front of her.

"What?" she said, defensively.

Michael continued to stare at her. "You've got that stuff on your lashes," he said, a little surprised.

"No, I don't."

He got closer to her.

"Yes, you do. You know that stuff girls put on their lashes to make them look longer or something."

Grey nudged him away. "You mean mascara?"

"Yeah, that stuff."

"So?"

"So, nothing. I think it looks . . . pretty."

She looked away. "Shut up."

"What? I'm serious."

"Whatever." Grey pushed Michael out of the way and walked past him, wanting the conversation to end.

Grey and Michael walked in silence.

Grey had never been one for makeup. Mom rarely wore makeup. Grey admired this and thought she was beautiful just the way she was. When Mom put makeup on, it was minimal. She didn't understand why some of the girls at school wore so much makeup.

Grey could feel her heart beginning to beat a little faster as they approached the bonfire. The smokiness of the burning wood drifted in the air, and she could hear the beating drums trying to find a cohesive rhythm. The sun dipped below the horizon and the barely there, transparent moon awakened in the sky. There was an energy present that excited Grey.

Grey and Michael walked around the bonfire, weaving in and out of the crowd. Grey's eagerness grew. Would she see Zale? She glanced around, nonchalantly, trying to be cool. She didn't see Zale or anyone he was with last Sunday. She was a little disheartened, but it was still early.

She looked over at Michael who stood quietly next to her. She didn't know how to begin a conversation with him. She didn't want him to think she was angry with him because she wasn't. She really loved her brother. He had always been there for her whenever she needed him. He always tried to explain things to her when she didn't understand something or when she didn't *want* to understand something.

Michael had patience with her and accepted her for exactly who she was. He understood her. He was being nice about the mascara, but she was embarrassed. She felt so awkward at times; sometimes like an adult, sometimes a child. She hated that whenever she would do some little thing differently, Mom or Michael would notice and make a big deal out of it. She just wanted to go unnoticed. That's what she thought . . . until she met Zale.

Someone offered Michael their drum. He smiled, shrugged his shoulders, and joined in, sitting right down in the sand. Grey admired that he could fit in anywhere and would try anything. He had that sort of charisma people were drawn to. She was proud to have him as a brother. She watched as he pounded on the drum trying to find a beat with the others. He looked over at Grey. Grey couldn't help but return his smile.

Grey watched for a while and then walked down to the water's edge to get away from the crowd. She let the water touch her toes as she watched the moonlight beginning to reflect on the water, moving with the current. It swayed remarkably with the beat of the drums.

"Grey," a voice called out softly.

She stiffened. Her heart raced. *Could it be?* She slowly turned around to see Zale standing in front of her. The flames from the bonfire illuminated his figure, making it appear like he had a halo around him. He seemed otherworldly to Grey.

He tilted his head to one side. "I thought it was you." He took a step toward her.

Breathe. She got lightheaded . . . *Breathe.* She hated it and loved it at the same time.

"I wasn't sure if you would be here," he said.

"Hi," she managed to say.

"Are you alone?" he asked.

"No, I'm here with Michael. My brother," she added.

"I was hoping you would be here tonight."

"Oh?" she replied shyly.

"I didn't really get to talk to you last Sunday."

"Yeah, I had to leave," she said, looking down at the sand, squishing it with her toes like she had before.

"So, what are you doing here?" he asked.

"What?" she asked, her heart sinking.

"I mean, what are you doing *here*." The corners of his mouth curled upward as he outstretched his arms, referring to the area they were both standing in. "All alone."

"Oh," she said, laughing nervously, relieved she misunderstood him. "I just wanted to get away from the crowd for a little while."

"Yeah, it can be a bit much."

Grey smiled.

"You're new here," he said.

"Yes."

"Are you here for the summer?"

Grey nodded.

Zale smiled. "I see."

"And you?" Grey managed to ask.

"I've been here for quite some time."

"Oh . . . you're lucky."

"I don't know if luck was involved." He seemed distracted. "Anyway," he continued, quickly changing the subject. "I would like you to meet my friends."

Grey managed to hold his gaze for a few moments and then looked down. When she looked at him again, he was surrounded by his friends. Grey was a little taken aback. She had only looked down for what seemed like a few seconds. Where did they come from so quickly . . . and so quietly? She didn't hear them approaching, yet there they stood, surrounding him, just like last weekend.

They were perfect, their hair, their skin, their bodies. They gracefully stood looking at her with their heads tilted. Waiting. Staring. Except for the one on the end who was reading a book. Grey looked at Zale who was smiling. Was he going to introduce her to them? What was he waiting for? She was beginning to feel uncomfortable and a little intimidated. Where was Michael? Suddenly she felt very far away from the bonfire and everyone there.

"I'm sorry, Grey. Forgive me," Zale finally said.

He gestured with his hand to the right. "This is Newel." She stood with her hip cocked to one side. Her combat boots planted firmly in the sand. Her legs were perfectly white and flawless in their cutoff denim shorts, unlike her own leg with its big scab on it from her adventures in the woods.

She lowered her head and smiled deviously. "Hello."

"Hi," Grey shyly replied.

"And Lars," he gestured to his left. Lars' spiky blond hair was a contrast to his dark eyes.

"Hello," said Lars, coolly.

Grey shyly smiled, acknowledging him.

"And next to Lars, is Minna."

Minna stopped reading her book, casually leaning her arm on Lars' shoulder. Her tall slender body was angled in a way that only models seem to do with ease in fashion magazines. Her long white hair looked almost fake, so shiny and perfect. "Hello," Minna said, a little aloof, staring down at her as if it was a bother.

"Hi," replied Grey.

Minna went back to reading her book, still leaning on Lars, ignoring everyone.

Grey's stomach began to churn. Zale's friends didn't seem to like her very much. *How was she going to get out of this?* She wanted to stay and talk to Zale, but it was clear that his friends didn't like her. Finally, Grey summoned the courage. "I should go find Michael."

"Maybe I should come with you," Zale said.

Grey slowly shrugged her shoulders. "If you want to." Should she say something to Zale's friends? But they were just staring at her, except for Minna, who was engrossed in her book. *What a warm reception.* Grey began to walk away.

"Grey, wait," Zale said.

Grey stopped.

"Minna, the book," Zale said with his hand outstretched, not taking his eyes off Grey.

Minna continued reading the book, ignoring Zale.

"Minna, the book," Zale said, a little stronger.

She shot Zale a look. "I'm not finished with it."

"You know how it ends," he said, his expression growing dark.

After a moment, Minna rolled her eyes. She walked to Zale and dropped it into his opened hand.

"Here." He handed Grey the book. "I think this is yours."

Grey was confused. Slowly she took the book from Zale. It was her copy of *Romeo and Juliet*! She was stunned. "How?"

"Come on, let's go find Michael," Zale replied, nonchalantly walking toward the bonfire, leaving his friends behind.

Grey, dumbfounded, looked at the book in her hand, and

then at Zale, who was a few steps ahead of her, quickening her pace to catch up to him.

"How did you get my book?"

". . . Ahhh, *Romeo and Juliet*, one of the darkest love stories of all time."

"Zale, did you see me in the woods?" Grey blurted out, taking a step closer to him.

"In the woods?" he asked, feigning confusion, a slight smile coming across his lips.

Grey nodded.

"When was this?"

"About a week ago."

"What was I doing?"

"Leaning against a tree."

Zale's smile broadened, amused by Grey.

"In the rain," Grey continued, seriously, as she looked at him.

"You have a great imagination," he said, smiling directly at her.

His smile made her weak. "There is that opening or clearing at the quiet end of the key, surrounded by those beautiful white trees and . . ."

By the look of amusement on Zale's face, he wasn't going to admit he was there.

She wasn't going to push it. She knew what she saw. She could never forget those piercing blue eyes or his hair for that matter. She had never seen anyone like him before. It was like he reached out and touched her on that day, and that feeling she experienced in that moment, would stay with her for the

THE BOOK OF ETERNITY

rest of her life.

"The woods, in the rain . . . with you? It sounds nice," he said as he clasped his hands behind his back, not going any further.

"There's your brother. I will see you soon, Grey."

Grey clutched the book to her chest.

"My bounty is as boundless as the sea, my love as deep," he said looking into her eyes as he walked backward away from her.

"The more I give thee, the more I have, for both are infinite," she said softly, finishing the quote from *Romeo and Juliet*, unable to take her eyes off him.

He did see her. He was there. She knew it!

"Hey, where were you?" Michael ran up to her.

Grey was watching Zale.

"Hello!" Michael said, waving his hand in front of her face.

Grey looked at Michael.

"Where were you?" he asked again.

"I was talking to Zale."

Michael turned around, but there was no one there.

Chapter Nine

The night was calm. Zale peered down through the skylight, watching Grey sleep peacefully in her bed. She slept on her back with her face toward the French doors. The white sheets were neatly pulled up to her chest. Her copy of *Romeo and Juliet* laid on her night table. The moonlight shone down on her, caressing her face. Zale reached out and softly touched the skylight with his fingertips, wanting to reach through and touch Grey. *Who was this mere human who was so simple and young yet had such strength that she was allowed to touch the Book?* he wondered.

"What are you doing, Zale?" a voice said behind him.

Zale knew that voice all too well. It was just a matter of time until this little visit occurred.

"Breel. What took you so long?" Zale smiled as he turned around.

Breel was the same height as Zale and had the same slender build. He stood in the glow of the moonlight, his straight blond hair brushing his shoulders. His angular jaw relaxed as he stared at Zale.

"I've been watching you." Breel's voice was calm.

"I've noticed," Zale said. "The 'Leader of the Almighty Surge' is watching me . . . What a surprise." Zale laughed.

Breel took a step toward Zale.

"You lied to the girl when you told her you didn't know us at the beach."

"A mere technicality. What's your point?" Zale asked, glancing down at Grey through the skylight.

"You cannot do this." His voice was laced with a tone of authority.

"Whatever do you mean, 'I cannot do this?' Surely you jest," Zale said, playing with Breel.

"You feel you are entitled to her soul."

"I am."

"She is an Innocent."

"She is, and she is my freedom."

"This must be a mistake."

"I have control now. Full control. How much does that bother you?"

"You will not hurt that girl," Breel said, calmly.

Zale laughed. "What makes you think that is what I'm planning?"

"Zale, Leader of the Fallen. You would never walk away from an opportunity for a soul and certainly not one that would free you of your . . . malediction. What other reason would there be for you to be interested in a human? You have such distain for them."

Zale chuckled. "Malediction. Oh, come now. You are so dramatic." Zale turned and walked away from Breel.

"What I don't understand is . . . why are you wasting time getting close to her? I would think you would want your freedom." Breel sounded suspicious.

Zale did not respond.

"You watch her," Breel continued.

"I have my reasons."

"This is another one of your tired games."

"Perhaps . . . but it is mine." Zale sighed.

"I will not play your game."

Zale turned and faced Breel. "Oh, but you already are. You're here, aren't you? You are concerned for the girl. That is what you do. You care about humans," Zale said with disgust.

Breel's eyes were locked on Zale. "I have known you long enough to know something is different here. I just can't quite put my finger on it."

"She touched the Book. It's that simple."

"That is right, she touched the Book. What harm has it done?"

"What harm has it done?" he said, raising his voice. "You are so amusing." He smiled. "Now that the tables are turned, Breel, the One Who Intercedes, comes to grovel."

"This is a mistake!" Breel shot back.

"It is no mistake. This is the rule. You and I have known about this for centuries," Zale replied, calmly.

Breel walked toward Zale. "I will not have this!"

Zale did not flinch.

"Let me remind you that Neema, one of yours, dropped the Book and Minna, one of mine, had to pick it up. This is the Surge's fault, not ours," Zale said, angrily.

"No harm has been done," Breel argued.

"You know the consequence. I get to destroy, with my bare hands if I choose the Innocent who will break the curse. It's purely euphoric." Zale threw his hands in the air.

"She is an Innocent. Sixteen years old."

"And that is what we are."

"We are centuries old."

"Not in their eyes," Zale reminded him. "You're always trying to save humans," he said as he shook his head.

"That is what I am here for."

Zale outstretched his arms. "This is what was *supposed* to happen."

"But not like this . . . Zale, the great leader of the Fallen," Breel taunted, "on his knees, being nothing more than a mere human. I think there is more here."

Zale put his hands in his pockets. "You are grasping at nothing, Breel," Zale said, coolly.

"You will not touch her," Breel said with authority.

"I already have," Zale smirked.

"You have not!" His voice rose with anger.

"In my own way, I have," Zale said, slyly.

"I am calling a meeting before dawn between the Fallen and the Surge at the Crest to discuss this."

"We will see," Zale challenged.

"You do not want to start this," Breel shot back.

"It has started," said Zale turning his back and defiantly walking away from Breel.

"We were once the same."

Zale stopped. He looked up at the black sky gleaming

with stars and took a deep breath. "We just came from the same place," Zale reminded him.

"We were on the same side."

"That was a long time ago." Zale began to walk away again.

"We were friends. We stood side by side."

Zale stopped. After a moment he turned to face Breel. His face was solemn. "We were, but we are very different now."

"And that's okay."

"It's not, and you know it."

Breel took a few steps toward Zale. "You didn't have to do it."

Zale looked down and shook his head. "Ahhh, but you see, I did. We were here before humans."

"It's sad that you saw it that way."

"You were more tolerable than I . . . You never questioned."

"I didn't have to."

"You didn't feel what I felt."

"Anger, betrayal?"

"You weren't looking for what I was."

"Zale, you were given the power among us, but you wanted more."

". . . and you were content." Zale laughed.

"You fell, like lightning from above."

Zale's smile faded as he stared at Breel. "I didn't fall . . . I was thrown."

"You were impeccable, full of enlightenment, and allure just like the one before, whom you chose to follow."

Zale stared at Breel. "So does that make one stronger

THE BOOK OF ETERNITY

or weaker?"

Breel locked eyes with Zale. "You were from the highest order of Angels, the Cherubim."

Silence. Zale turned and began walking to the edge of the roof.

"We will always protect each other!"

"Until we can't." Zale disappeared into the night.

"I am sorry," Neema stepped out of the darkness behind Breel. Her long brown hair hung straight, framing her delicate face, making it seem paler than it really was.

"It is okay, Neema. Get the others and meet me at the Crest," Breel said, concerned.

Chapter Ten

The Crest was quiet as streaks of bright moonlight found their way through the dense canopy of trees. Breel stood at one end with Neema and two others.

"It is no one's fault, Neema," Breel said.

"It is all my fault," Neema said.

"It's not." Micah ran his fingers through his spiky hair.

"I will be the reason an Innocent loses her life."

"That will not happen," Breel assured her.

"I am sorry. It slipped from my hands when the humans came to the Crest. I heard them and hid like everyone else, but as I was above them going into the trees . . . I . . . I dropped it. I didn't know what to do," she said.

Breel could feel the weight of the situation on Neema's shoulders.

Murial stood next to Neema, trying to comfort her. She put a long willowy arm around Neema's shoulder. Her long brown hair pulled back at the sides, making her appear as if she were from another time.

"The Fallen will gain another soul," Neema said sadly.

They heard rustling behind them. Breel quickly turned around.

The Fallen, Zale, Minna, Newel, and Lars, stood in the center of the Crest.

The members of the Surge stepped away from the trees. They stood in silence.

"So, why are we here?" Zale broke the silence.

Breel stood strong and stared at Zale. "You know why we are here."

Zale let out a long sigh as he slowly walked to the left of the clearing.

"What do you want from me?" asked Zale.

"You know what we want."

"We're here and you are wasting our time," said Zale.

"You have the time of eternity," Breel said.

Zale smiled slyly. "I do, but she doesn't."

The members of the Fallen snickered at this.

"Always so dramatic." Zale laughed.

"She is an Innocent! She didn't do anything wrong!" exclaimed Neema, unable to control herself.

Zale waved his hand. "Oh Neema, always trying to save them, is that what this gathering is all about? We already had this conversation Breel."

"We want your word you will not harm the Innocent," Breel said.

"She touched the *Book of Eternity*, wherein all celestial and earthly knowledge is set down!" he reminded them, his patience wearing thin. "The Book has the laws of eternity, the laws of humans, of why they exist, how they were created. Of

Heaven and Hell!" Zale seethed through clenched teeth.

"Do we have to remind you that if the Book is ever touched by a human, that human must be destroyed?" Minna remarked with a coy smile.

". . . and we get their soul," Zale said with a devious smile.

"That is only if a human touches it with evil intentions. Individuals since the beginning of time have searched for the Book for power, for personal gain, evil reasons, to start wars," challenged Murial.

"She is my freedom. The exception. One purely innocent soul to free me," said Zale.

"We don't know what her intentions were," Lars pointed out.

"The Innocent's intentions were pure. She didn't know what she was touching. She didn't do it for euphoria for eternity, or to unleash the secrets of all time, or to gain anything," Neema said, clenching her fists. "She didn't even know what it was."

Minna shrugged her shoulders. "Human beings and their curiosity."

"Always treading where they don't belong," added Lars.

"Always ruining the balance," said Newel, coldly.

"What can you do?" Zale sighed.

"That is what they are supposed to do," said Murial.

"To live their lives. That is their reason for being here: to test boundaries and make discoveries," said Micah.

Breel stepped toward the Fallen. "That is what you are doing right now!" Breel reminded them. "You are testing the laws of the book. You are drawing others in and creating a world, a situation, chaos, and we," he said, gesturing to him-self and the Surge, "are all being drawn in, to flesh out the order again."

"Are you comparing us to humans?!" Zale asked, annoyed. Breel smiled at him.

"How dare you compare us to humans!"

"Oh Zale, we are not unlike humans," said Breel.

"How dare you say that! We are nothing like them," Zale said. "They are the chosen ones. Remember?" he said, with sarcastic anger. "We are mere trash, thrown to the side," he continued, bitterly.

"This is not true," Breel said calmly.

"Yes, it is," Zale fought back. "You, however, are the Surge. You are glorified," he said with bravado as he walked around Breel, raising his arms to the sky.

"You had a choice and you made it," Breel said. "You chose to embrace the darkness. You live by another set of rules, and you always cause unrest because you enjoy it."

"We are all different. This is what makes our world . . ." He walked nonchalantly past Breel.

"Interesting," replied Zale.

Breel turned around to face Zale, anger rising in his voice. "This is their world—this is where they belong."

"That's right, 'Their world,' not ours. So, why would you expect me to behave like them? I am not of this place, and neither are you, so stop pretending!" Zale warned.

"You mean to bring pain to her!" Neema cried out.

Zale turned, smiling deviously at Neema. "I mean to do more than that. I mean to do what is my right," he said in a low, vicious growl.

"You are sick," Newel replied, disgusted.

"Thank you," he said, smiling.

Breel had not taken his eyes off Zale throughout this theatrical display.

"Why do you watch her sleep?" Breel asked calmly.

The smile quickly faded from Zale's lips. He turned swiftly, shooting Breel a vicious look with eyes that were solid black. In a split second, he was face to face with Breel.

"What?" he seethed.

"I saw you tonight watching her sleep. Why do you do this if you plan on doing her harm?" Breel asked coyly, not intimidated by Zale's change.

"You watch her?" asked Minna, a hint of anger in her voice.

"I have my reasons, and they are mine alone." Zale never lost sight of Breel as he ignored Minna's question.

The Surge, amused by this, watched Minna. Her eyes locked on Zale.

Breel walked around Zale and whispered in his ear. "If I didn't know you so well, I would think you cared for this one . . . this human."

"Watch your words," he hissed.

"Why are you getting so close to her? Are you intrigued by her courage? The courage that you don't have?"

He resented the direction Breel was going with this. Zale could feel Minna's cold stare and knew he had to come from a position of power.

"Do you yearn for her . . . strength?" asked Breel.

"I yearn for nothing!" Zale roared, as he turned to face Breel.

"You yearn for her!" Breel shot back, his eyes as black as Zale's.

"YOU DO NOT KNOW ME!" Zale screamed, as he shot straight up into the night sky . . . there he hung . . . still. His form now changed. His once perfect skin marred by bluish veins, pulsating with fury just below the surface. The skin on his back split to release three sets of black, feathered wings, spanning six feet on each side. His teeth grew long and pointy, and his once perfect nails grew long black talons. Hands, now discolored, clawed the air. He glared down upon Breel. "How dare you assume my thoughts!" he bellowed, swooping down at Breel who stood perfectly still, unmoved by Zale's display of anger.

Breel gracefully shot into the air. Zale turned to see Breel above the Crest. Breel's perfect white skin shone white and translucent. Three sets of white, feathered wings with black tips, spanning six feet on each side, were now revealed. His nails protruded, long white talons with black tips. Teeth, bore long and pointy like Zale's, but pure white. There he hovered in the middle of the Crest, staring at Zale.

"Because I know what you are thinking!" Breel said, the wind blowing fiercely, forcing the leaves to be torn from the comfort of their branches.

Zale, with one swift thrust of his wings, propelled himself across the Crest immediately face to face with Breel.

"You do not know what I am thinking!" Zale's voice was so guttural that it shook the earth. The Surge and the Fallen needed to steady themselves.

"I do!" Breel shot back, the wind engulfing them. "Your assumption is your ignorance! That is your downfall!"

"You know nothing!" Zale's guttural voice continued to shake the earth. "I have my plans for her. I have already claimed her! The penalty is death, and we get the soul! ONE INNOCENT SOUL TO FREE ME!" With that, Zale pulled back his great wings and drove them down forcefully, shooting himself up. The branches of the trees parted, and he disappeared into the night sky.

Minna raised her face and let out a long screech. Her arms were outstretched and shaking. Breel looked down at her, unfazed, his wings pulsating ever so slightly. She finally stopped out of sheer exhaustion. Her chest rose and fell as she gritted her teeth before turning and disappearing into the woods. Lars and Newel shot the Surge menacing looks before turning and following Minna.

Quiet.

"Boy, is she pissed," chuckled Micah.

Murial smiled.

"I'm afraid he is right." Breel stood in front of them in his human form. "The soul of any human who touches the Book goes to the Fallen."

"But this is the first time it's been an Innocent," said Neema.

"Yes, yes, it is Neema."

"What do you think he will try to do to her?" Neema sounded concerned.

"I don't know." Breel shook his head.

"Do you think he will wait until the Copper Moon?" asked Micah.

"I believe he will. He is, how should I put it . . . very hands on."

"No! We need to stop him before he does anything to the Innocent." Neema's voice rose with anxiety.

"It seems like he is going to play with this one first," replied Micah.

"He is so cruel," Neema said, distraught, as she sat down on the grass.

Breel walked to the other end of the Crest where Lars and Newel had disappeared and stared into the forest. He was quiet. He clasped his hands in front of him, keeping them close to his body, as he often did. The Surge watched Breel as he stood, motionless, staring off into the dark woods.

Neema, Murial, and Micah looked at each other. They were all thinking the same thing; they couldn't remember the last time they had seen Breel like this. They knew this was serious, and it would be a fight.

Neema hung her head as she sat on the soft grass. Micah and Murial lowered themselves next to her, waiting for Breel to say something.

"We have six nights until the Copper Moon. He can't physically touch her until then," Breel finally said. "That is the only time Zale is allowed to physically touch humans," he continued, still staring into the darkness of the woods.

"There are other ways he could harm her without touching her," Murial said, concerned.

"Yes, yes there are," Breel replied solemnly.

"You don't think he'll try to do anything before the Copper Moon because he wants something from her?" asked Murial.

Breel turned around to face the Surge. "That's what I'm thinking, but what?"

"Her brother was terrified. He could barely move when they were here at the Crest, and he saw the *Book of Eternity*," Murial said, thinking out loud, as she stretched her long legs out in front of her.

"Why do you think that is?" asked Micah.

"I don't have that answer." Breel sighed. "There is something I need to tell you." He knelt in front of them, his blond hair falling forward around his face. "I had hoped over the centuries that this day would never come. That I would never have to say these words . . . but . . . this Innocent may be different." He folded his hands on his lap.

"Different?" asked Neema.

"A long time ago, an order was set forth, a deal if you will, between Heaven and Hell, whereas an Innocent would be sent, having the ability to touch the *Book of Eternity* without any earthly consequences. We were not told in what form, man or woman, young or old, we were just told, an 'Innocent'—they would be known as the One."

Neema, Murial, and Micah listened intently.

"Whoever this was, would not want anything from the Book. They would not know why they were drawn to the Book, nor would they seek out the Book and want what the evil kings, rulers, politicians, and others had wanted over the centuries: to conquer, obtain more money, bigger armies, power, greed, etc. This 'Innocent' would not want anything . . . but they would be sent for a specific reason . . ." Breel stopped for a moment, looking down at his hands. He sighed heavily before he looked at them, almost unable to go on.

"The reason: The Fallen would gain one purely innocent soul . . . not only to free Zale of his curse, but the One would unleash the fury of Heaven and Hell and begin the Celestial War."

"Grey, as we know right now, can free Zale of his curse. But we don't know if she is the One. The One needs to be destroyed by Zale and Zale only. They will turn to dust and will not exist even on a celestial level. The soul will be no more, a 'true death' . . . but there is something else." Breel looked up at the night sky and pursed his lips. He lowered his head and looked at the Surge.

"The Celestial War would begin and eventually wipe out the world as we know it."

Neema's eyes filled with tears.

"A war between good and evil. Not to be fought on earth, by humans, but to be fought by us . . . all the Angels. This is when death is possible for *us*. The fight to finality. There would be no more celestial or earthly laws or rules to obey. In the end, the world would be left unbalanced; all good or all evil. Humans would never be able to exist in such a place. Any human who miraculously survived our war would eventually die. The world would be barren of all living things. Nothing would exist."

"Like it used to be," Micah said.

"Yes, like it used to be. A lonely, dark time void of life and light . . . there is a chance Grey may be the One," Breel said solemnly.

No one knew what to say.

"No more humans . . . What would our purpose be?" Neema asked, breaking the silence, a tear running down her face.

"Our purpose, I'm afraid, would be gone."

"No, this can't be," Neema said with despair.

"Why was this order created?" Micah asked, disheartened.

"This was created in the beginning . . . when Zale was cast out."

"Why weren't we told of it?" asked Murial.

"Because it came well before all of you, and there was no need for you to exist with such a burden."

"This really is all my fault!" Neema sobbed.

"It is no one's fault, Neema," Breel said gently. "The wheels were set in motion a long time ago. You did not create the order. Remember, Zale was the first to want to leave. With one blow, he was cast out of Heaven, sent into the unknown, and taken under the Mentor's wing. After him there were others, but he was the first. He set the precedent. Zale introduced evil to humans by dispersing it here on Earth. Through the centuries, he has had time to learn many things and hone his craft. He is cunning. A master of disguise."

Neema wiped her tears away with the back of her hands. "Why does he watch her?"

"That I don't know. It is very unlike him," replied Breel.

"Maybe he sees some of himself in her," offered Micah.

"This is a possibility . . . her strength maybe," agreed Breel. "This one is different for the obvious reasons, but I think there is more. I have known Zale for centuries, and whatever it is, it seems to be throwing him off, maybe intimidating him. I don't think he is aware of it. That is dangerous. The last time he experienced anything like this was when he was cast out."

"But I thought he wanted to be cast out?" Neema said.

"He did, but once the gravity of what he had done sank in, he became unsure of himself. Frightened and confused until he was taken under the Mentor's wing. Then, and only then, did he feel safe, like he had a home again. He regained his strength and confidence, creating and becoming, the leader of the Fallen."

"Maybe he is curious about her," said Murial.

"She is so powerful, and she has the freedom to touch," Neema said, softly.

Breel looked at her. "Yes, to touch," he said.

No one said anything. Breel knew they were trying to process what they had just learned.

"Zale, the only one of us who cannot touch a human unless the Copper Moon is out," Breel finally said, breaking the silence.

"Wanting to touch what he hates . . . but also, I think, what he may secretly aspire to be." Neema's voice broke.

"Because he thinks they are above him and more important than him," Murial whispered.

"That's a horrible punishment," Micah remarked.

"It's sad," Neema said softly.

Breel was quiet. He looked down and gently ran his fingers through the soft grass.

"I don't think Zale is thinking this Innocent could be the One, otherwise he would have said something about the Celestial War. His mind is clearly elsewhere."

"How do we know if she is the One?" asked Murial.

"We don't. There is no way to know. That was part of the agreement, a sort of Russian roulette, if you will."

"My concern at this moment is Minna. She may try to possibly bring harm to Grey now that she knows Zale watches her."

Neema, Murial, and Micah looked at Breel, distraught.

"Should we make contact?" asked Murial.

"Yes," said Breel.

Chapter Eleven

Dawn was barely awakening on Sleepy Key as Minna, Lars, and Newel walked through the woods close to the shore. The transparent moon hung in the sky, soon to be just a thought. There was anger in Minna's stride. She stomped her combat boots into the earth, walking at a maddening pace, dry foliage and scrub crunching furiously under her feet with each step.

"What is wrong with you, Minna?" Zale asked abruptly, standing in front of them.

"Nothing." She pushed past Zale.

"Fine. Then will you slow down?" Newel asked.

Minna stopped and spun around, stopping Newel and Lars in their tracks. She pointed at Zale, teeth clenched. "He watches her."

"So?" said Lars, fluffing it off.

"So? So?!" Minna shot back, in disbelief.

"Minna, it doesn't mean anything," said Newel.

"It means everything!" Minna yelled, causing the ground to shake.

Lars steadied himself. "This is not the first one he has watched."

Zale leaned against a tall tree and looked up at the pewter-colored sky.

Minna paced. "He watches her sleep. This is different. She is different, I knew it when he took her book from me and gave it back to her. I could feel it."

"I am surprised you feel this way." Lars smiled. "He is toying with her, Minna."

"No, he is not. There is something there," she argued.

"He is just having fun. We all are," said Newell. "He's ruffling the feathers of the Surge, making them agonize over the Innocent. So much fun."

"Making Neema feel worse than she already does," said Lars, laughing. "Right Zale?"

Zale smiled and nodded.

Minna looked at Zale, shaking her head. "No."

"Minna, do I have to remind you that this is what we do?" asked Lars.

"We cause trouble and that is fun." Newel jumped up on a tree stump.

"And then we watch . . ." Lars smiled.

"It's wonderful." Newel laughed, pirouetting on the stump.

"They are right. I am surprised at you, Minna," Zale said, nonchalantly. "After all this time. I thought we knew each other better than that." He let out a long sigh.

"Why do you watch her?" Minna asked, suspiciously.

Zale walked over to Minna. "Why do we have to go through this?"

"She is a human."

Zale threw his hands up.

"She is different."

"Why is she different, Minna?" Zale asked, a hint of exhaustion in his voice.

"You heard Breel," she said. "He was right."

Zale turned away from Minna.

"You are intrigued by her because of her courage," she continued.

"Don't listen to Breel," he said. "Don't you see what he is doing? He is trying to get us to argue so they have more time to figure out how to save the Innocent."

"I'm not convinced," Minna replied, standing her ground.

"He's right, Minna," said Lars.

"And it's working. We're wasting time," said Newel.

"When will you destroy her?" Minna asked.

Zale turned to face them. He put the extended index fingers of his clasped hands to his lips as if he was deep in thought. After a moment, a smile came across his lips.

"During the Copper Moon, dear Minna. You know it is the only time I can touch a human. I will gain the freedom to touch . . . but I want to use my bare hands with this one. Afterall, she is the only Innocent to touch the Book . . . ever."

Lars and Newel smiled at this. They understood Zale's plan.

"And what will you do?" asked Minna.

"You know what I will do. You have known me for centuries. You know what I am capable of." Zale swaggered closer to her with that wicked smile on his face. Minna began to soften.

"Come on, Minna," Lars said, "Zale's right."

"Yeah, Minna," Newel said, sitting on the stump, growing bored.

Zale lifted Minna's chin in his hand. "We don't have much time. We can't fall into their trap. It just distracts us from what we need to do . . . Add a little misery to their perfect existence."

Minna tilted her head, looking into Zale's eyes. "Are you sure?"

"Minna, she is a human," he reminded her as he slid his hand from her chin to her waist, moving his body closer to hers. "She is what we have rallied against for centuries," Zale said, disgust rising in his voice. "Have you forgotten that?" he asked her, their lips almost touching.

"You're right." Minna said. After a moment, her demeanor changed. Minna leaned into Zale and put her mouth to his ear. "What if she's the One?" she whispered.

Zale froze.

Chapter Twelve

$\mathfrak{I}$didn't see it!" Mom yelled from the kitchen.

Great. Grey opened the door to her room. How would she ever finish her summer reading if she could never find her book? She looked around and walked across to her nightstand. She distinctly remembered putting it there last night. *Why do I keep losing my copy of Romeo and Juliet?* She made it a point to leave it in her room because when she took it out last time, she lost it. She still wasn't sure how Minna got the book. She must've been at the Crest because Grey was positive that was where she lost it. Things were very strange. She looked everywhere. She got on her hands and knees and looked under the bed, just in case. Nothing. Leaning back on her heels, she let out a long, exasperated sigh.

"What are you doing?" Michael stood in the doorway.

"I can't find my *Romeo and Juliet*."

"Again?"

Grey pushed her hair out of her face.

"Do you think Mom—"

"Don't even think about it, Grey. It's probably the

most important thing she has left from Dad," he said, and walked away.

She sat on the floor. Through the sheer curtains, she saw something that was out of place. She strained to make out what it was. The outline looked like a person sitting at the table. She was startled but curious. Who was it? It couldn't be Michael or Mom.

She got up and slowly walked over to the doors. She peeked through the curtains and there she saw Zale sitting at the table! Her heart beat faster! *Oh my God! It was him!* After a moment, she opened the French doors. Zale looked up at her with those piercing blue eyes that made her weak.

"But, soft! what light through yonder window breaks?" he said softly.

Grey was confused.

"*Romeo and Juliet*," Zale said, holding up the book.

It was her book! She wanted to ask him what he was doing, sitting on her deck, but honestly, she didn't care. She was so excited to see him, and she couldn't believe he was there. She held onto the door handle for dear life. He had such confidence, but it was a quiet confidence, in an almost shy kind of way. She admired it and was drawn to it.

"My book." She gestured toward it.

"Yes." Zale held it up. "It's one of my favorites."

Grey looked down at her feet, her head swimming.

"Do you like it?" he asked.

"What?" she asked, barely able to look at him.

"The book," he said as he raised it.

Grey fidgeted with the door handle. "Oh, uh, yeah. Well,

I haven't finished it yet."

"It's the first time you're reading it?"

"Yes." She squeezed the door handle harder, twisting her foot into the wooden deck.

"I've read it thousands of times," he said.

Grey gave him an odd look. "Thousands?"

"Well, it seems like thousands. I'm sure it's less than that," he said, catching himself.

Grey closed the door and leaned against it.

"You always seem to have my book."

"I do, don't I." He smiled.

"Yes, you do," she replied. Grey loved his smile. His teeth were so perfect and white.

The moon shined so bright that she could see her book being cradled in his hand. His hands were flawless. They weren't too feminine, and they weren't too rough. What would it feel like if he held her hand in his?

"I don't know how that keeps happening," he said.

She smiled at him.

He extended the book to her, inviting her to come closer.

She hesitated for a moment and then walked over to the table and took the book from him. She sat in the chair across from Zale, placing the copy of *Romeo and Juliet* on her lap.

"I hope I'm not disturbing you," Zale said.

"No," she said, looking down at her book.

"Because I can leave if you would like."

"No, it's fine," she said, trying to play it cool, the sound of her beating heart pounding in her head.

She put her book on the table and pulled her knees to her

chest. Her mind raced as she tried to think of something to say. Finally, she thought of the obvious. "How did you know where I lived?"

Zale was looking down at his hands, and after a moment, he replied, "Oh, I have my ways." He looked up at her with a seductive smile.

"Oh." That wasn't the response she was expecting at all. She looked out over the ocean and up at the moon.

"The moon . . ."

"It's so bright," she said.

"Yes. It gets quite bright here, and it's not yet a full moon," he said.

"I wonder when that will be."

"There will be a full moon in five nights. It will be a Copper Moon."

"What's a Copper Moon?" asked Grey.

"It happens once a month just like a full moon, but here, off the key, it's bright copper."

"Wow, it must be beautiful." She looked up at the moon again.

"Anything is possible when the Copper Moon is out," he said, looking right through her.

What did he mean by that? She was beginning to perspire. The heat from the day lingered into the night. Zale seemed to be fine. He wasn't sweating. That was weird. Not only was he beautiful, but he didn't even sweat.

She wanted to ask him again about seeing him in the woods that day, but she just couldn't bring herself to do it. It had been haunting her since she asked him at the drum circle.

"Grey?"

She looked at Zale.

"What are you thinking?" he asked.

She hesitated. Should she ask him? She wasn't sure she had the nerve. "Nothing."

He looked at her for a moment, leaning his elbow on the table and resting his chin in his hand. "I find that very hard to believe."

Grey took a deep breath. Why was this so hard for her? She looked away.

"I saw you in the woods," she said, getting her courage up. "Did you see me?"

Zale smiled a devious little smile. "This again?"

She waited for an answer.

"Maybe I did, and maybe I didn't," he said.

She knew he saw her! She smiled. She couldn't help it. He had the best smile. Mesmerizing.

"Grey?"

She froze. Who was calling her?

"Grey?"

Oh no! She thought. *It was Mom!*

Panic came over her as she turned around toward the French doors. The shadow of Mom walked through her room toward the deck. She wasn't sure what Mom would do if she found her with Zale alone so late at night. Would she embarrass her? Would she yell at her? Surely, she wouldn't be happy!

The French doors opened. Mom looked at her. Grey braced herself for the embarrassment that was coming her way.

"What are you doing out here by yourself?" Mom asked.

"What?" Grey asked nervously, trying to figure out a reason she would be alone on her deck with a boy Mom had never met. *Wait, did I hear her right? By myself? But Zale* . . . She turned around. The chair was empty. He was gone!

"Are you okay?" Mom asked.

"Uh, I, um . . ." Grey stumbled, confused, looking at the empty chair where Zale was sitting.

Mom put her hand to Grey's face. "What's the matter?"

"Nothing. I'm fine," she said, trying to figure out what just happened. Zale just vanished. Not a sound. Nothing.

"Is there anything you want to talk about?"

". . . No, I'm fine," Grey replied, still preoccupied.

"You don't look fine, Grey," Mom said, concerned. "You look a little . . . you look like you're distracted."

"No, really Mom. I'm fine," Grey said, relieved that Mom hadn't seen Zale.

"Are you sure?"

"Yeah."

"I'm always here if you want to talk about anything. I know things have been . . . They've been different," Mom said carefully.

Grey looked at Mom. "I know."

"Alright, well, Michael and I are going to watch a movie. We wanted to know if you would like to join us."

Grey was looking at the chair Zale had been sitting in. *Where did he go?*

"Grey?"

"What?"

"Do you want to watch a movie with us?"

"Um, sure, I'll be right there." She really didn't want to watch a movie. She wanted to be left alone.

"Great," Mom said happily. "Oh, did you find your book?"

"What?" Grey asked, still preoccupied.

"*Romeo and Juliet.* Did you find it?"

"I did. I found it on . . ." She looked on the table where she put the book, and it was gone. ". . . the table."

"Good. You should really be more careful where you put things." Mom walked back into Grey's room.

He took her book again! She couldn't believe it! She had no way of finding him because she didn't really know anything about Zale. If he read it so many times, why did he need her book? Didn't he have his own copy? On the other hand, she thought it was kind of cool that he took her book. It was like she had a connection to him. But when would she see him again?

She walked to the edge of the deck and peered down. Nothing. He was gone. She turned around and leaned on the deck. Again, she looked at the chair Zale sat in. She smiled at the thought of him. How did he leave so quickly . . . and so quietly? *Anything is possible when the Copper Moon is out.* Oh, the sweet dreams she would have tonight.

Chapter Thirteen

ou're joking, right?" Michael asked with a hint of sarcasm in his voice. They put their bikes on the bike rack outside the small Village Grocery Store.

"No. I'm serious Michael," Grey said.

"He just appeared on the deck last night," Michael said, a hint of doubt in his voice.

"No, he didn't just appear. He was sitting at the table."

"Yeah . . . and?"

"And what?"

"What happened?" Michael asked.

"That's not the point. The point is, he just disappeared when Mom came out."

"Disappeared?"

"Michael, he was there. I turned around. Mom came into my room, and when she walked out onto the deck, he was gone. It was a few seconds."

"So? Maybe he jumped over the railing like I do." He chained the bikes to the rack.

"No. He didn't make any noise."

"Maybe he's used to skipping out on girls quietly," Michael chuckled.

"Michael!"

"I'm just saying. Look, Grey, he's a total stranger. You don't know him, and I'm not crazy about him. He wouldn't shake my hand that night on the beach. . . Weirdo."

"He is not a weirdo!" Grey protested.

"He's a weirdo. He can't even knock on the front door."

"So what?" Grey shot back.

Michael gave her a look of exasperation.

"Fine. Let's go. Let's get Mom's groceries." She walked toward the door to the quaint Village Grocery Store.

Grey was insulted by Michael's comment. Zale wasn't a "weirdo." She thought it was romantic that he was on her deck. It reminded her of *Romeo and Juliet*. The deck was her balcony, and Zale came to her. He quoted from the book to her . . . "But, soft! what light through yonder window breaks?" Was he comparing her to the light? So romantic! Who cares if he didn't knock at the front door. She was happy that he didn't because it would have been so awkward having to introduce him to Mom, who probably would have tried to have a conversation with him and invite him to watch the movie. So embarrassing.

"Let's walk around first," Michael said, unaware that he had hurt Grey's feelings.

"Alright," Grey conceded.

They walked past open-air restaurants that were already buzzing with people, bars with music playing and people dancing. There were small shops ranging from funky jewelry stores to surf and tourist shops that sell T-shirts, towels, and beach-themed knickknacks.

"This is totally different from the other side of the key," Michael said. He watched the cars cruise by.

"Yeah, you're not kidding." Grey watched the tourists and beachgoers leisurely walk along the tiny sidewalks.

"This is cool." Michael smiled.

There was life on the key.

Everyone rode bicycles and cars cruised by slowly. People smiled or said hello to Grey and Michael. It was different from what they were used to. It was barely lunchtime, and this end of the key was already full of life. She liked the feeling here. It wasn't lonely, and it felt safe. Safety was something she hadn't felt in a long time.

The village was only a few blocks with streets that veered off and looked like they all held a secret. The houses were each different too. They were older, but in a cool way, and they each seemed to have a story to tell. The chipping paint and the vines that crawled up the walls added mystery to the homes.

Michael pulled the front of his T-shirt away from his body to give himself some relief from the heat. The sun was strong and there was not a cloud in the sky.

"Let's get something to drink." He playfully pushed Grey in the direction of a coffeehouse.

Grey laughed as they stumbled into Regular's Coffee House, a small off-beat, place with an open-air feeling. The walls were painted a bright yellow and the tile floor was pastel green. They walked up to the dark wooden counter, where they were greeted with a smile by a petite blonde around Mom's age.

"Hello!" she said. "What can I get for you?"

"Two iced teas, please," Michael said.

"Sure. Please have a seat if you'd like while I make them."

They walked over to a dark wooden table for two up against the wall by the front door and sat. They browsed through various magazines that were in a basket on the floor for the customers to read. A few people in the café seemed to be regulars and knew each other. Grey liked the sense of community. A lot of people had dogs.

"Your iced teas are ready," the petite blonde called out in a friendly voice.

Michael got up, paid for the drinks, and brought them back to the table. Grey was thumbing through a magazine when Michael put her drink in front of her. A little black dog with a white streak on the top of its head and one white paw trotted over to Michael. It sat down before looking up at him.

"Hey there," Michael said, reaching down to pet the dog.

Grey looked up from reading the magazine to see Michael halfway under the table.

"Michael, what are you doing?" she asked, looking under the table. "Oh, how cute," she said. She reached out to pet the dog when she noticed four sets of worn black combat boots walk into the coffeehouse. The boots looked familiar to her, and one pair had red ribbons for laces, which she had seen before but couldn't remember where.

Michael was sitting on the floor now, playing with the dog, totally oblivious to everything. Grey was fine to hang out under the table until she could figure out where she had seen those red ribbons before.

Think, think! She was drawing a blank. Why couldn't she remember? It wasn't like she knew anyone around here. She kept petting the dog to buy herself more time.

"Excuse me." she heard a guy's voice say.

"Oh sure." replied Michael, as he moved out of the guy's way.

"Thanks," the guy replied.

Michael picked up the dog and sat in his chair, putting the dog on his lap.

Grey couldn't stay under the table anymore, so she took a deep breath and slowly sat up in her chair, keeping the magazine in front of her face. She took a sip of her iced tea as she hid behind the magazine and carefully peered over it. She saw two girls and one guy at the counter, but they had their backs to her, so she couldn't see their faces. There was something very familiar about them, but she couldn't figure out what it was.

"This is the coolest dog ever." Michael said, rubbing the dog behind its ears as the dog just laid in his lap looking up at him with his big black eyes. Grey smiled as she watched her brother and the dog.

"Hey Shadow," a male's voice said.

The dog stood up in Michael's lap, wagging its tail.

"Is this your dog?" Michael asked.

"Oh no. It's my sister's dog" The man gestured to the petite blonde behind the counter.

Grey slowly lowered the magazine and looked at the guy. He smiled at her. She froze, remembering where she knew him from. He was with the group she saw on the beach at the drum circle that Zale said he didn't know. They had caught her eye because they were so beautiful and unique, and she thought the red ribbons for laces the girl with the brown hair had were cool.

"I'm Breel." He rested his hand on the back of Michael's chair.

"I'm Michael, and this is my sister, Grey."

She could do nothing else but stare at him.

"Hello, Grey." He smiled.

Another perfect smile. "Hi." Her hand quivered slightly as she reached for her iced tea.

A girl walked up to Breel and handed him a drink. "Hi, I'm Neema," she said, in a soft voice. Her long brown hair hung down over her white tank top and almost reached her cut-off denim shorts. Grey looked down—there were the red ribbon laces.

"Hey, Shadow," another girl said, kneeling in front of Michael to pet the dog.

"This is Murial," said Breel.

"Hi" Murial said, with a smile as she pushed her auburn hair out of her face.

". . . and this . . ." he said, turning around, ". . . is Micah. This is Michael and his sister, Grey."

"Hey. I see you've met Shadow." Micah smiled.

Grey could feel Breel staring at her. *They sure were friendlier than Zale's friends.*

"I've seen you before," Breel said to Grey. "Where was it?" He tilted his head to the left which caused his hair on the right side of his face to perfectly caress his cheek.

Grey forced a smile and shyly shrugged her shoulders. "I don't know."

Breel continued staring at her and tilted his head to the right, taking a long sip from his straw.

"Didn't we see her at the drum circle a couple of weeks ago?" Murial asked, still playing with Shadow on Michael's lap.

Breel slowly nodded his head. "That's where."

"Yes. She was talking to Zale, right?" asked Micah.

Wait! The smile slowly faded from Grey's lips. *Zale said he didn't know who they were. He lied!* Her heart dropped. She tightened her grip on the magazine in her hands.

"Yes, that's where I saw you." Breel gracefully pushed his long blond hair behind one ear with his fingers.

Grey forced a smile.

"Hey, we're having a party Saturday. You two should come," Breel said.

Michael took an excited look at Grey. "Yeah, that sounds cool."

"Great," said Murial.

"Zale will be there," said Breel.

Michael rolled his eyes at Grey.

"Will you come, too?" asked Breel.

"Umm, maybe," she finally said, overwhelmed.

"She'll be there," said Michael.

Grey kicked Michael under the table. He quickly pulled his leg away giving her a dirty look.

"Let me give you the address."

"Here, put it in my phone." Michael handed Breel

his phone.

Breel typed it in and handed the phone back to Michael. "It starts around eight," Breel said, smiling at Grey.

"Sounds great," said Michael.

"See you then," Breel replied.

Just then, Michael's phone rang. He jumped. Breel laughed.

"I wasn't expecting it to ring. I haven't had any service."

"Yeah, it's sketchy here." Breel pulled his phone out of his back pocket. "We rarely have service. See?" He showed Michael his phone. Michael shook his head and smiled. "You better answer it while you can."

"Yes," Michael answered the call. "Hi, Mom." He listened for a moment.

Grey watched as Breel, Neema, Murial, and Micah walked to the back of the coffeehouse followed by Shadow who pranced with his tail up. They disappeared through a doorway with hanging beads.

Michael hung up the phone. "Milk. She didn't want us to forget the milk."

Grey put the magazine back in the basket. "Come on, let's go." They took their iced teas outside. "You just had to say I would go to the party, didn't you?" she said, punching him in the arm. "What's wrong with you?"

"Whaaat?" he said, rubbing his arm.

"Maybe I don't want to go."

"Yeah, right," Michael said, sitting on a bench in the shade. "Zale is going to be there. You're not going to go? Please."

"Be quiet." Grey watched as the condensation from the plastic cup dripped on her leg, tickling her as it ran down to her calf, and disappearing into her sock.

"So, you're not going to talk to me now?" he asked.

"Zale said he didn't know them," she thought out loud.

"What?" Michael asked, confused.

"When I was talking to Zale at the drum circle the other night, he seemed to be distracted by something. So, I turned around, and I saw Breel and his friends. Zale said he didn't know them. I didn't ask. He just said it. But he does know them. Why do you think he would lie?"

"Who knows. He's a weirdo, like I said."

Grey looked at her brother who was looking at her squarely in the face, and they both cracked up.

Michael leaned back on the bench. In the distance, faint music floated through the air from the outdoor bars. "So, do you want to see him again?"

Grey furrowed her brow. "Who?"

"Who? Who are we talking about? Zale."

"Oh, I don't know . . ." she said, taking a sip of her iced tea. ". . . I guess . . . If he's at the party, I won't have a choice." She smiled coyly biting on her straw.

Michael laughed. "You knew you wanted to go."

"No, I wasn't too sure." Grey smiled.

"Well, you know you can always find him at the drum circle," said Michael.

He always teased her. Grey leaned back on the bench. She hoped this was true, and it gave her something to look forward to.

Chapter Fourteen

Michael rode into the garage on his bike with Grey behind him. They noticed an old red convertible sports car in the driveway that clearly didn't belong to anyone they knew.

"Whose car is that?!" Michael's eyes widened.

"I don't know," Grey replied, a little suspiciously. She heard the front door to the house open and she jumped off her bike. She ran to the edge of the garage and looked up the steps of the house.

"Thank you for coming by. It was so nice to meet you," Mom said from inside the house.

"Same here, and thank you for the lemonade," a female voice replied.

Michael took the grocery bags out of his basket and started to walk out of the garage as the girl came down the steps. He was eager to see who had such a cool car. Grey pulled him back into the garage.

"What?" he said.

Grey put her finger to her lips and shook her head.

"I want to see who it is."

"We can see from here," Grey whispered as they peeked around the garage.

The girl walked to her car with her back to them. She opened the door and turned to get in, taking off her hat as her long blonde hair tumbled down to her waist. Grey gasped and quickly pulled Michael back into the garage.

"What is wrong with you?" Michael asked, annoyed.

The color had drained from her face.

"Grey?"

"That's Minna!" Grey hissed.

"Who's Minna?"

"Zale's friend."

Michael peeked around the garage to see Minna's long blonde hair blowing behind her as she peeled out of the driveway. "Can you introduce me to her?"

"I would never do that to you." She took the grocery bags out of her basket, pushing past her brother to make her way up the front steps.

"Why not?" Michael asked, as he quickly caught up with her.

"Because," Grey said, opening the front door.

"Because why?'

"She's not your type," she snapped, quickly walking to the kitchen, Michael on her heels.

"Hey Mom, we're home!" she yelled.

"Why not?" Michael pressed.

"Mom?" Grey called out, concerned. They put the bags on the kitchen table. "Where is she?" Grey asked.

"I don't know. She's gotta be around here somewhere, and since when are you so concerned about her anyway?" Michael said.

"Shut up," she said, scrunching up her face at him.

She ran upstairs into Mom's room. Nothing. She ran back downstairs and into the kitchen. Now, where did Michael go? The groceries were just as they had left them. She heard a scream, She ran out the French doors that led from the kitchen to the deck. She leaned over the deck to see Michael holding the garden hose, and Mom, who was fully clothed, soaking wet, lying on the lounge chair. Michael was laughing hysterically.

Mom laughed as she said, "Michael, look what you did to me!"

Grey began to laugh too. Michael and Mom looked up at her. She ran down the steps. Michael turned around, aiming the hose at Grey. She put her hands up to protect herself from the spray of water as she ran toward Michael. Mom ran over too. They wrestled with Michael until they finally got him close enough to the pool to push him in, but instead, they all went in. They came up laughing. The hose was lying on the ground, spraying water straight up into the air.

"Look, a rainbow," Mom said, out of breath.

There was a rainbow in the mist of the water spraying out of the hose. "Wow, look at that," replied Grey.

"Thanks to me," said Michael.

Grey splashed water at Michael.

Michael hugged Mom. Grey looked at them. She couldn't remember when they both looked so happy. It felt good to see them this way. This moment reminded her of Dad. He was a prankster just like Michael. She always figured that was where Michael got it from. If Dad was here, he would be in the pool with them, clothes and all.

It was times like these when she was reminded how much she deeply missed him. She wished the four of them could all be together again. Her eyes brimmed with tears.

"Did you remember to get the milk?" Mom asked.

Grey shot Michael a look of panic.

"The milk!" Michael yelled. "We forgot to put it in the refrigerator!"

Michael jumped out of the pool, grabbed a towel off a lounge chair and raced up the steps taking them two at a time.

Grey and Mom laughed as they watched Michael disappear into the house. Mom looked at her, and their laughter faded; Grey looked away, suddenly feeling awkward.

"I forgot to tell you, your friend Minna was here right before you got home," Mom said gently.

Grey froze. Minna was *not* her friend.

"She seems very nice."

"Oh, um, what did she want?"

"She was looking for you."

"She was?"

"Yes. She told me all about how you two met at the drum circle."

Grey watched an ant run along the pool coping before disappearing in a small crack in the cement. "Oh, yeah."

"I'm sorry you missed her. She said to text her or give her a call."

Grey didn't respond.

"Grey?"

"I will. Thanks, Mom."

Grey was suspicious. She had no idea why Minna was at her house, but she didn't like it.

"Is there anything you want to talk about?"

Grey turned to Mom with tears in her eyes.

"Oh, Grey . . ." Mom went over and hugged her. Grey held onto Mom until she stopped crying. She took a step back and wiped her tears with her hands.

Michael barreled down the steps with two platters of food. "Come on you, guys. Let's cook. I got chicken and some vegetables. We are going to have some barbeque." He placed the food on the small table next to the grill.

They both stepped out of the pool. Grey looked down and saw her clothes clinging to her body. "I'm going to get changed." She wrapped a towel around her and handed one to Mom.

"Me, too," said Mom.

"I'll set the table when I'm done," Grey said, drying herself off.

"I'll help you."

"That's alright, Mom. I'll do it." Grey walked up the steps to the upper deck and went inside. She quickly changed into her bathing suit. She would be prepared this time in case Michael decided to play games with the hose again. She walked into the kitchen and got some paper plates, a pile of napkins, and utensils, and walked back outside onto the deck.

Grey was setting the table on the deck when she heard

cooing. She turned around. A mourning dove perched on the railing of the deck just a few feet away. It looked at her and cocked its head from side to side. "Hello, little bird," Grey said.

It cooed back at her.

Grey smiled at the bird. It didn't seem to be afraid of Grey.

Mom opened the sliding glass doors and walked out onto the deck.

Grey turned around. "You put your bathing suit on too?"

"I wasn't taking any chances." Mom set a pitcher of iced tea on the table.

Grey turned to see the mourning dove still perched on the deck railing, cooing.

"Oh, how cute!" Mom said, making her way back into the house.

"It's been hanging around."

"The barbeque is hot and ready," Michael yelled up to them.

Grey opened the umbrella above the table to block out the sun, still strong in the late afternoon. She went back to setting the table, making sure the napkins were folded just right before walking to the railing of the deck and leaning over. She watched Michael put the food on the barbeque. He was purposely dropping the chicken on the grill so the flames would shoot up. She shook her head. He always found ways to amuse himself. It didn't matter what they were doing.

Mom stepped out onto the deck. "Michael, be careful. I don't want you to burn yourself."

"I won't, Mom." He grinned.

Mom laughed and shook her head.

"Do we have any barbeque sauce?" asked Michael.

"I think we do. I'll get it," Mom said, and went back into the house.

He dropped the last piece of chicken on the grill and closed the lid.

Grey laid down in a lounge chair while Michael and Mom tended to the barbeque. She shielded her eyes from the sun and watched the seagulls gracefully glide and dive in the air. Her eyes began to feel heavy. She closed them, listening to the crackle of the barbeque and the waves gently crashing on the beach. Soon, she was lulled to sleep.

"Grey!" Michael called.

She opened her eyes. How long had she been sleeping? She could smell the smokiness and tell that the food was almost done. Groggily, she saw the mourning dove on the railing pecking around at the wood, occasionally looking up at her. It appeared as if the bird were watching over her.

"Grey!" he called out again.

"What?" she said, annoyed.

"Come here."

She was so comfortable. Why did he have to bother her? Grey reluctantly got up and walked to the railing of the deck.

Michael gestured toward the beach with his head.

Grey looked out. She didn't see anything. "What?" She leaned on the railing of the deck with her head in her hands.

"On the beach!"

Grey scanned the beach. She looked at Michael, shrugged her shoulders and mouthed, "What?"

"You're really blind." He pointed to the left of the beach, just at the point where a person's view would be obstructed by the shrubbery.

Grey narrowed her eyes, looking toward where he was pointing. She gripped the deck a little tighter. Her toes twisted into the wood of the deck. Was it really him?

By this time their mom had also seen what Michael had seen, or rather, *who* Michael had seen. "Who is that?" she asked Michael.

"Ask Grey, that's her friend," Michael said as he turned a piece of chicken.

She didn't know what to do. Should she walk over to him or stay where she was? Should she pretend she didn't see him?

Grey heard cooing again and turned around. The mourning dove was right next to her on the deck railing looking up at her, frantically tilting its head from one side to the other. If Grey didn't know any better, she would have sworn the little bird was trying to distract her. "Grey, who is that?" Mom yelled.

Oh no, what would she tell Mom? Grey didn't really know who he was, so how could she explain it to her? She looked down at Mom. "Oh, uh, I don't know," she blurted out.

"Yeah, right," Michael said, smirking as he put the cooked chicken on a platter.

Grey looked out to the beach again . . . but he was gone. Her heart sank a little, but she was also relieved.

"Not only does he not use the front door, but he lurks in the bushes too," said Michael.

Grey came down the steps.

"Knock it off, Michael," she said.

"Grey, who was that?" Mom asked again.

"Just someone we met at the bonfire."

"Zaaaale," Michael said, stretching out his name.

Grey shot him a look.

"What?" He walked past Grey with the platter of chicken.

"Does he live here?" Mom asked.

"Who knows where he's from," Michael replied. "He's weird."

"He does live here," Grey protested.

"He likes her. He thinks she's beautiful," Michael chimed in, and walked up the steps.

"Shut up, Michael." Grey turned her head away, embarrassed by his teasing.

"Okay, you two. Stop it," Mom said, trailing them.

Michael put the chicken platter on the table and sat down. Grey sat at the table, glaring at her brother.

"Now, I want the both of you to eat your vegetables." Mom put the dish down on the table and opened up the foil to reveal a steaming mix of carrots, asparagus, and potatoes.

Grey made a face at this. *Yuck, they're all mixed together.*

"Don't make that face," Mom said. "I had to do it quickly, and this was the easiest way."

"I think it's great, Mom." Michael dug in.

Grey reached for a piece of chicken and put it on her plate. She looked out over the beach in the direction where Zale was standing and wondered why he was there and where he went. She pulled the skin off the chicken leg and put it on the side of her plate. *Why did he think she was beautiful?* The girls he hung around with were beautiful. A little snobby, but beautiful, nonetheless. He must really feel this way because he told Michael. He wouldn't tell her brother something like that if it wasn't true, would he? *No, he wouldn't,* she decided. She bit into the chicken. It was moist and had that perfect smoky, grilled taste to it that she loved so much. Comfort food.

"Grey? Grey?"

She looked at her mom, her mind still lingering on her thoughts.

"So, are you going to tell me about this boy?"

Michael smiled at Grey as he shoved some vegetables in his mouth.

"Michael," Grey warned.

Michael put up his hand in protest while trying to chew and swallow his food quickly. "I didn't say a word," he said after swallowing his food.

"You didn't have to," Grey said as Michael chuckled.

She scowled at him. "It's not funny."

Mom was looking at her, waiting for an answer.

"Look, it's no big deal. I really don't know much about him, like Michael said," she explained, shooting him a look before he could say anything. "I met him at the bonfire and then we ran into each other again the following week." Her mother was waiting for more. "That's it, Mom." Grey put another piece of chicken in her mouth as she squinted her eyes at her brother.

"We're invited to a party Saturday night," Michael interjected.

"A party? Whose party?" Mom asked.

"Oh, this guy Breel and his friends."

"And how did you meet these people?"

"At Regular's."

"What's Regular's?"

"It's like a little coffeehouse or café in town. You should go, Mom. It's really cool."

"When did you two go there, and why don't I know about any of this?"

"Oh, when we went grocery shopping for you today. We walked around town for a while and stopped and got iced teas."

Michael was always so forthcoming. She finished the last of her vegetables.

"So, you really don't know these kids," Mom said.

Here it comes.

"Well, no, but Grey saw them at the bonfire. Apparently, they're friends with Zale."

Grey was going to kill her brother! What a big mouth he had sometimes.

"Do you know them, Grey?"

"Ahhh . . . not really." Grey took a long sip of her water. "Like Michael said, they're friends with Zale."

Mom shook her head. "I don't know. You don't really know who this Zale boy is, so . . ."

"It will be fine, Mom." said Michael. "We'll be together, and we'll ride our bikes so we can leave whenever we want to."

"Where is it?"

"I don't know," Michael replied, "But it's on the key somewhere."

"Well, I'm not sure about the party. We'll talk about it later."

She rolled her eyes at her brother.

"Grey, will your friend Minna be there?" Mom asked.

"You really need to introduce her to me," Michael said, smiling.

Grey shot her brother a look. "I don't know, Mom."

"Well, maybe you should call her and find out."

"Hmm."

"Oh, and Grey, you know what Minna did before she left? She hugged me. Who does that these days?"

A soft cooing caught their attention. They turned, and the mourning dove took flight off the railing of the deck.

Chapter Fifteen

The mourning dove fiercely flapped her wings, only allowing herself to gracefully glide through the air when the wind would carry her. She had to reach the others immediately.

The Surge were gathered at a table on the outdoor patio in the back of Regular's. It was a quaint, hidden oasis where varied flora and fauna intertwined up and over the walls and into a trellis overhead, which let in the bright sky of day and the star-filled night.

The mourning dove landed on the ground in front of the Surge, tucked her wings underneath her and seamlessly transformed into Neema, her long brown hair gently blowing in the warm breeze.

"He was there," she said, trying to catch her breath. "He was watching her from the beach."

Micah and Murial looked at Breel, their brows furrowed with concern.

"I want you to stay close to her, Neema," instructed Breel. "He is unable to detect you in your other form. But be careful, because in your other form, you are vulnerable to him, and if he senses anything suspicious . . . he can and will cause you harm," Breel warned.

"I know, I will be careful," Neema said with certainty. "But there is something else . . ." she added.

"What is it, Neema?" Breel asked, seeing the concern on her face.

"Minna went to Grey's house."

There was silence. This was not what they were expecting.

"You saw this?" Breel asked.

"No, Grey's mom told her. She said Minna hugged her."

"What!" Breel said, shocked, as Murial and Micah gasped.

"I came here immediately when I found out."

"Was Zale with her?" Breel asked.

"No, she was alone."

"So, he must not know," Micah said.

"What are we going to do?" Neema quickly said.

Breel stood up and began to pace. "This can't be. Zale will be furious."

"Why would she do this?" Murial asked, concerned.

"I don't know," Neema said, sadly.

"Okay, at least we know what she has done."

"We need to surround them and watch," said Murial.

". . . and help when the time comes," Micah added.

"Yes. That is what we will do. We will stay very close to them," Breel said.

Breel quickly put up his hand to quiet them. Everyone was still . . . Then, the beads in the doorway parted.

"I hear you're having a party?" Zale swaggered onto the back patio with the Fallen.

"We are," Breel confirmed as he sat down at the table.

Zale glanced over at Neema. "Out of breath Neema?"

Neema held his gaze.

"Well, this is very interesting . . . So, what are you crazy kids planning?" Zale plucked a pink flower from the vine that crawled up the wall.

"Planning? What do you mean?" Breel asked, innocently.

"Don't waste my time." Zale's upper lip curled with disdain.

"If we told you our plans this wouldn't be your game, now, would it?" Breel ran his finger along the table in front of him.

Zale smirked and turned his attention to the flower he was twirling between his fingers.

"Why are you trying to get us all together?" Minna asked, with a slight tone of anger in her voice. ". . . and with humans."

"To have a party," Breel said, calmly. "We so rarely all hang out." He smiled.

Zale laughed at this.

". . . And considering that Zale made contact with the humans, it is only fair that we invite them," he said, staring directly at Zale.

"We have our own plans for them," Minna said, unable to control herself.

Zale shifted his eyes from the flower to Breel.

"It's just a game. It will be fun," Zale said, walking away. He stopped. "I do find it odd, however, that you have chosen to have a party on the night of the Copper Moon." He held his hand up for everyone to see and watched the flower in his palm turn to dust. "Dust . . ." He blew the remains from his hand. ". . . just like the Innocent."

Chapter Sixteen

rey stood on her deck with her elbows on the railing looking out over the ocean. She was grateful that she had her deck to escape to. She liked that she could be outside without having to actually leave her house. This afforded her extra space from her mom too, who Grey felt was encroaching more on her privacy. She watched the moon's reflection sway on the water. The warm breeze gently blew strands of her hair across her face. She let them linger there until she couldn't take it any longer, brushing them away.

She wondered where Zale was. There was something mysterious about him, something she was drawn to aside from the way he looked. It was deeper than that. Intangible.

"Who are you?" she whispered out loud, listening to the mesmerizing sound of the palm trees blowing in the gentle breeze.

"I know not how to tell thee who I am," a familiar voice said from below.

She froze. Her heart pounded with excitement. She leaned over the deck railing but didn't see anyone.

"My name, dear saint, is hateful to myself, because it's an enemy to thee."

His voice came from behind. She turned around quickly. Zale stood staring at her with his right shoulder leaning against the house.

"Zale," she whispered so low she thought he wouldn't hear it.

"Grey," he whispered back.

"How did you get—" she started to ask.

"Why are you always out here by yourself?"

"I'm not always out here by myself."

"It seems like you are," he said, tilting his head to one side. "You like to be alone, don't you?"

"No," she said, thinking about how Zale could make it so quickly onto her deck when he was clearly just in the garden two levels below her. "Well, sometimes."

"I thought so." The corners of his lips ticked upward.

He seemed to understand her. The thought was comforting because she felt no one understood her, and she was in a constant free fall because of this.

"Were you always like this?" he asked, smiling.

"Like what?" she asked, trying to buy herself more time to come up with an answer.

"Guarded, like you have a shield around you," he replied.

Grey looked at him. "No." Grey responded. *Why did he want to know anyway?*

"Don't you want to be free? Free to wander and discover?"

There was no answer from Grey.

"What happened that took you to this place?" he asked.

"What do you mean?"

"I was just thinking that something must've happened for you to want to spend so much time by yourself. It's like your armor," Zale probed, still leaning against the house.

"I don't know." Grey shrugged, turning away from him, and walking across the deck.

"You don't want to tell me."

Grey didn't reply. She looked up into the night sky, unsure if she was ready to share that story with him.

"That's okay," Zale said, pushing himself off the house and slowly walking toward her. He stood a few feet away, leaning on the railing of the deck, looking out into the night sky. "We all have secrets."

Secrets? What secrets? She came to be this way after Dad died, but she didn't consider that a secret. It was something personal that she didn't feel she had to share.

Zale turned his head and looked at her. "Talk to me," he whispered.

"About what?"

"Tell me a secret."

"I don't have any secrets to tell."

Zale gave her a sidelong glance.

"Tell me one of your secrets," she blurted out, surprising herself.

Zale smiled. "One of my secrets . . ." He turned away and walked to the other side of the deck. " . . . Let's see . . . I know what it's like to be alone. To feel different." He spun around to face her.

Grey was thrown for a moment. She wasn't expecting that level of honesty from him. "You do?" she asked softly.

"Yes."

"How?" she gently asked, wondering how this beautiful boy could ever possibly know what it's like to be alone or feel different. He seemed to have it all.

"I was alone for a long time because I was different. I'm still alone."

Grey hesitated for a moment. "Don't you have a family?"

"I do," he said, nodding.

"If you have a family, how can you feel alone?"

". . . Even though you have a family you can still feel alone. Don't you feel alone sometimes?"

She had never really thought about it that way. "I guess."

"See?"

"What about your friends?"

"It's the same thing. You can have friends and still feel alone. It's weird, you know?"

Grey was relieved that someone else felt the same way she did.

Zale watched her as she pondered what he had said. "This is not a game Grey. I want to feel closer to you. I want you to share your thoughts . . . your feelings with me so we can be closer. I trust you. Do you trust me?"

Grey hesitated. "I do."

"We both have pain . . . pain that no one else understands." He stepped closer to her.

"How do you know I have pain?" she pressed.

"Because I do, and I know when someone else does. I can feel it."

Zale looked at Grey. It was the first time she held his gaze without turning away.

"My father didn't want me," he said. "He threw me out. I was made to feel like an outcast, a stranger. I wasn't worth anything to him. No matter what I did, I couldn't please him . . . as much as the others."

He looked so vulnerable to Grey, as if he was suspended in time, all alone in the universe. She softened. She found herself wanting to protect him.

"I'm sorry. Do you talk to him?"

"No, he wants nothing to do with me."

"What about your mom?" Grey asked, cautiously.

He shook his head before looking away.

"Give me your pain," he whispered, his gaze locked on hers.

Grey tried to push the thought of Dad away because this wasn't something she really wanted to get into now, but the memories of him were flooding her mind one after the other. The more she pushed them away, the faster they came. She couldn't control them. She felt the overwhelming urge to run.

"You have a weight on your shoulders. I feel it. I know it, Grey. Let me take your pain."

She walked to the other end of the deck. She couldn't believe Dad was gone. She could hear his voice, his laugh. She wanted to talk to him. She wanted to touch him and hug him and have him hug her back. She missed that so much. She missed feeling safe, knowing everything was going to be okay.

Her heart was heavy, her throat ached. She couldn't control the tears that filled her eyes. This was the last thing she wanted to happen in front of Zale.

"I want to help you, Grey," he said, taking a few steps closer to her.

A single tear streamed down her face, and she quickly wiped it away. Grey realized how tired she was. She didn't talk to anyone about what had happened to Dad. It was exhausting carrying that around. She found her mind constantly replaying the events of his five-year fight against death. That's exactly what it was—a fight against death. She couldn't control it. When she came to Sleepy Key, she had fleeting moments where she didn't think of him constantly. The guilt she felt from this was enormous. When this happened, she was worried that she was forgetting about him but deep down inside she would never forget about him. It was an up and down ride of emotions that exhausted her.

"My dad," she whispered, barely audible, fighting back the tears.

"What about your dad?"

"He's not here . . ." She lowered her head as she covered her mouth with her hand.

Zale didn't say anything.

"He died." She struggled to fight back the tears. That was the first time she had ever said those words out loud.

"I'm sorry, Grey."

She turned to face him. "Why should you be sorry?" she said defensively, hiding behind the shield she built around her.

"Grey . . ." He took another step toward her.

"No," she said, raising her hand to keep him away. "It's so weird. At first everyone says they're sorry and they want to hug you. They think it will make things better, but it doesn't. And then, people treat you differently . . . like you have a disease or something. They avoid you, and you hear them whispering behind your back. They feel bad for you. I don't want anyone to feel bad for me . . . My dad was the one who went through everything. He's the one who had radiation and chemo. He's the one who had the pain . . . and he never complained . . . not once . . . and I guess I never realized how bad it really was because dads aren't supposed to leave."

Grey turned away. The emptiness enveloped her. She grabbed the deck railing to ground herself. "He always smiled when he saw us and tried to be happy so *we* wouldn't feel what he was going through. He was this amazing person. He was my dad. He laid in that hospital bed getting smaller and smaller . . . wasting away . . . until he couldn't even talk anymore . . . This man who was so strong, who was my hero . . . just stopped being." She choked back tears as she put her hands to her face. "I miss him. It's not fair."

Zale felt her agony. "If we share these things with each other, they become easier to deal with." he said, softly.

Grey nodded, realizing he was right, as she wiped away her tears. She was exhausted but also a little relieved. She felt a little lighter.

"One fire burns out another's burning. One pain is lessen'd by another's anguish."

Grey turned and looked at Zale, confused. He took a step closer to her.

"You haven't been reading *Romeo and Juliet* have you?"

"I can't because you keep taking it," she said, beginning to smile through her tears.

"You're right," Zale said, smiling.

Chapter Seventeen

Grey opened her eyes. Thoughts of last night flooded her mind. 'One pain is lessen'd by another's anguish.' She couldn't believe that she shared Dad's story with Zale. Did she really meet someone who understood what she was going through? She rolled over and looked out the French doors.

She could tell it was another beautiful day through the sheer curtains. She felt uneasy, restless. What was this? She rolled over again, frustrated. She didn't want this day to be here. She didn't realize how hard it would be. It was a day she wished didn't exist, and she wanted it to be over. Her and Michael's birthday. The first one without Dad. Anger rose as reality set in. Dad. Wasn't. There. She didn't know why she was feeling this now. Did the conversation with Zale the night before stir up feelings she had been repressing? She realized just how angry she was.

She looked at the clock. Ten thirty. Usually by this time, Dad would have come in singing some silly little song he had made up . . . which didn't seem so silly now . . . and behind him would be Mom and Michael, and they would dance around the room. When the song was over, they would all laugh, sit on the floor and sing "Happy Birthday." Then they would go downstairs, have a big breakfast, and open their gifts. How special those birthdays were, though at the time, she didn't think twice about them because it was just what they did.

There was a knock at her door before it opened a crack. Grey saw a hand come around the door and Michael's head pop in.

"Happy Birthday, sister!" Michael sang.

Then she saw Mom's head pop in.

"Happy Birthday, Grey!"

She sat up and forced a smile.

They came in dancing toward the bed singing an upbeat version of "Happy Birthday." They pulled her out of bed. She halfheartedly followed their lead, dancing with them around the room.

The song ended with Michael singing an operatic "Haaaappy Biiirthdaaaay toooo us!"

The three of them fell on the floor, Mom and Michael laughing. Grey smiled at them. The laughter subsided and the happiness slowly turned bittersweet. They looked at one another with hope that the awkward moment of realizing that there was one person missing in all of this would some-how pass. Mom struggled to hold back her tears and Michael hugged her. Grey watched as tears filled her own eyes.

"He's laughing at us right now. You know that," Michael said, trying to hold it together.

"He would be so proud of the both of you," Mom said, wiping away her tears. "You're really good kids."

"Well, I am, but I don't know about her," Michael said, gesturing toward Grey as he laughed.

"Wait, I'll be right back." Mom pushed herself up off the floor and ran out of the room.

Grey and Michael looked at one another. They weren't expecting anything in light of what had happened to Dad. They knew, although they didn't talk about it, that they didn't have much money.

"Close your eyes," Mom said from the hallway before entering the room.

Grey and Michael closed their eyes.

She walked into the room and sat back down on the floor. Grey could hear the sound of her placing a gift in front of each of them.

"Okay, open your eyes!"

Grey and Michael opened their eyes and looked at the gifts in front of them.

She took a deep breath. She felt nauseated.

"Mom, you didn't—" Michael began.

"It's nothing big . . ." Mom trailed off, getting emotional again. She covered her face with her hands and nudged the gifts toward her children. She took a deep breath. "I was going to wait until later, but I think now is the perfect time." Her smile looked forced.

Michael opened his first. He picked up the neatly wrapped gift, carefully tearing the paper. When he saw the box, he stopped.

"I can't, Mom." He held the box out to Mom.

"Yes, you can," she said as she put her hand on his

shoulder. "Go ahead, open it."

He tore the last pieces of wrapping paper from the box and carefully held the box in his hands. Michael lifted the lid. It was Dad's watch. Michael turned it over and read the inscription to himself as his throat tightened. "With Eternal Love."

"He would have wanted you to have it."

Michael knew that Mom bought it for his dad when they got married and what it meant to Dad. "Thank you, Mom. It's the best gift ever . . ."

Grey watched Michael and Mom hug each other. He had loved that watch since as far back as he could remember. Dad held and rocked him when he was little, and the ticking sound put him to sleep. It was also the watch Dad taught him to tell time on. As they both got older, they came to realize how important it was to Dad—to both of their parents for that matter, and now it was Michael's.

He carefully placed it back in the box and looked at Grey who had her hands folded in her lap watching Michael.

Mom smiled at Grey. She lifted the gift and gently took the paper off. As soon as she removed the first strip down the center, she stopped. She looked at Mom as she fought back the tears. "Mom?"

"What's the matter?" Mom asked.

"Mom—" Grey didn't move.

"Please open it. I really want you to have it."

Grey hesitated, and slowly peeled the rest of the paper off.

Michael looked at the gift and then at her. "You better not lose that one," he said, half joking.

It was Mom's special edition of *Romeo and Juliet* that Dad

had given her when they got married. Grey opened the cover of the book and read the inscription to herself. "I am your Romeo, and you are my Juliet . . . I would die for you . . ."

She held the book to her chest as her eyes filled with tears. How ironic. She had read that inscription hundreds of times before Dad got sick but never realized the significance until now. This book was the Holy Grail to Mom, and now she understood why.

"Thank you, Mom." Grey awkwardly hugged her.

"I love you. The both of you," Mom said, grabbing Michael too.

They held onto each other tightly. For that moment, they were one unit, which they hadn't been in a long time.

"I miss him," Grey said softly as she slowly pulled away. She sat crossed-legged with her head down. Her hands were folded in her lap with the gift Mom gave her on the floor in front of her. She felt so alone at that moment.

"I know you do," Mom said. "I miss him too."

Grey shook her head. "I don't understand," she whispered.

Mom and Michael glanced at each other. This was the first time she had said anything to them about how she felt.

"It's not fair," said Grey.

"It isn't," said Mom.

"My world went away when Dad died."

"Oh, Grey." Mom reached out to touch her daughter, but Grey quickly pulled away.

"I'm so lost. I don't know who I am or why I'm here! Why was it him?" she asked. "Why wasn't it you?" She slammed her hands on the floor.

"Grey!" Michael yelled.

"Or me or Michael?" she continued, ignoring her brother.

"I don't know, Grey," her mom said, fighting back the tears. "I know you're angry, Grey."

"I'm not angry!"

"Grey, come on," Michael said, sternly.

"I'm sorry, but who do I get to blame?" she asked, and tears began to fall.

"No one, Grey. It wasn't anyone's fault," Michael said.

"No one? But especially not Mom's, right?"

"Why are you so angry at Mom?"

"It's okay, Michael." Mom reached for his hand.

"Whose fault is it, Mom? I need to blame someone." Grey's tears streamed down her face.

"There isn't anyone to blame," Mom said, trying to reach for her daughter again, but Grey pulled away.

"Why am I here? I don't want to be here," she said, shaking her head. "I want to be with Dad." Grey covered her face with her hands, crying.

"I know you miss him, Grey. We all do." Mom moved closer and put her arms around her. She held her, and finally she calmed down. She looked up at Mom who wiped Grey's face with her hands.

"Mom, what do I do with all of this . . . this horrible stuff I have inside?" she asked, softly. "I need to understand why this happened. And I don't."

"It takes time, Grey, and I know that's not the answer you want to hear, but it's the only truth I can give you."

"I would give anything to have him back," Michael said,

his eyes welling up with tears.

Grey looked at her brother.

"Me too," Mom said.

"He's only been gone for nine months, and I have so many questions for him and so much I want to tell him . . . I need him . . ." Michael's voice trailed off.

"He loved you two more than anything. You were his world, our world. Our hearts soared when we had the both of you." Mom wiped tears from her eyes. "Your dad taught the both of you a lot. You need to remember that and hold onto it."

"I know, but it's not the same as him being here," said Grey.

"It's not."

"Why Dad?" asked Grey.

"I don't know. I don't have that answer."

Mom reached for the box of tissues on the nightstand and put it in the middle of them. She took three tissues out, giving one to each of her children and used the last one to wipe her eyes. They blew their noses in what seemed like unison, looked at each other, and began to slowly smile.

Grey looked at Mom. Her body tensed. Mom was the sole provider now, which was something she hadn't given much thought to. Everything happened so fast when Dad got sick, but she and Michael didn't really feel the weight of it until the very end because Mom had really kept their lives as normal as possible. She never stopped. She took care of everything. She shielded her children from the dark side of the situation and never once complained. She would always say, 'You can't put a price on the time you have with the ones you love.' Now, reality was setting in.

"Come on, let's have breakfast," Mom said, trying to lighten the somber mood. "I'll make whatever you want."

"Anything?" Michael asked.

"Anything,"

"Hmmm . . . blueberry pancakes with scrambled eggs and bacon?"

"God, Michael, you're such a hog," Grey said, shaking her head.

They all smiled.

"Yes. If that's what you want, that's what I will make for you."

Michael and Mom got up and started to walk out of the room.

Mom turned around. "Aren't you coming, Grey?"

"Yes. I'll be right there," she said, looking at the book in her hand.

"Okay, but don't take too long. You know your brother. He'll eat everything."

"I won't," Grey said with a forced smile.

She was emotionally exhausted. She held the book to her chest. She thought about what it must have been like when Dad bought it for Mom. He had held this book so many times. She just wanted to hold it because he had.

Chapter Eighteen

Grey sat at the table on her deck. She watched as the faint silvery clouds slowly drifted across the nearly full moon. She liked the sound of the waves as they gently crashed on the beach and the way the light of the moon danced on the water. How lucky she was to be here.

She wondered what the party would be like on Saturday night and if Zale would be there. A smile came across her lips. Her breath quickened. What if Zale's friends were there and weren't nice to her? She wondered where he was now and what he was doing. What did Zale and his friends do on this tiny key? Where did they hang out? Was there some secret place that she wasn't aware of? The key seemed so isolated . . . beautiful, but isolated. Another world.

She looked up at the sky and thought about how infinite it was. She marveled at all the stars. She couldn't count them if she tried. When she was little and couldn't fall asleep, Dad would open the shade in her room, sit on the floor next to her bed, and they would count the stars. "Where are you, Dad?" she whispered. "I miss you, and I need you."

"Happy Birthday, Grey." She heard in a soft voice behind her.

She knew that voice. Her grip tightened around the arm of the chair, and her heart raced.

"You're watching the moon again," he said.

Grey didn't say anything. How did he know she was looking at the moon, she could have just been staring into the night sky . . . and how did he know it was her birthday?

"It's enchanting sometimes," he said.

Grey smiled.

"The Copper Moon will be in two nights," he said.

Grey felt him move closer. His proximity sent delicious chills through her body. Would he touch her? Would he just brush his face against her hair?

"This bud of love, by summer's ripening breath, may prove a beauteous flower when next we meet," Zale whispered so close to her ear that she could feel his breath.

She slowly turned around to finally look at him, expecting to be face to face with him . . . but he was gone. On the table was her copy of *Romeo and Juliet* and a red rose. She smiled, turning back to look at the stars.

She found him alluring. The way he came and went, it was almost like he wasn't real. She didn't bother looking for him because she knew he was gone. She reached for her book, the book that was once in Zale's hands. She ran her fingers along the cover and held it close.

"This bud of love, by summer's ripening breath, may prove a beauteous flower when next we meet," Grey repeated in her head. What did he mean by that? Was he saying that he loved her? That his love was a bud, meaning small or just beginning, and summer will turn it into a full-bloomed flower, like full-bloomed love? He couldn't feel that way for her after just a few weeks . . . could he? She loved how he made her feel, but was it love? Grey was confused. Happy, but confused.

Zale stood on the roof of Grey's house. He looked around at the treetops and wondered why he was there . . . again. How had he allowed himself to get to this place—to feel what he was feeling. Something was drawing him to her, and it wasn't in the way he wanted to be drawn to her. To any human. In all the centuries he had lived through, he had never felt this. He ran his hands through his hair in sheer frustration, tilting his head to the star-dotted sky. He listened to the waves crashing on the beach and stuffed his hands in the pockets of his long black jacket. He found the beach alluring at night when there was a good wind coming off the ocean. It made him feel truly alive.

The One? He thought to himself breathlessly. *Could she really be the One?* Why was he so intrigued by the Innocent? Was it because she was the key to his freedom, and possibly held the power to end the human race by starting the Celestial War? This Innocent was shrouded in mystery. It was as if he was blinded by her, unable to think straight. He was consumed by her.

He walked to the skylight, then stopped himself. He began to pace. He couldn't believe he was having this inner struggle. What exactly was it? She was human! He didn't like what was happening, yet he couldn't stop it. He should leave, but he couldn't bring himself to do so. This will be the last time, he told himself, because when the Copper Moon shines its redeeming light, he will show her what absolute hell is before he destroys her with his bare hands. He would not let a human get in the way of everything he had fought against for centuries. He would not let a human ruin what he had waited for since the beginning of time. When others took it upon themselves to play a cruel game with his existence, trying to humiliate him for centuries.

He quickly ran to the skylight, unable to contain his anticipation any longer, and got down on his knees. His hair fell forward as he peered down and gazed upon Grey. There she was, lying on her back with her face turned to the moonlight coming through the sheer curtains that hung from the French doors. The sheets were pulled up to her chest just like the last time. A human being. How was she able to touch the *Book of Eternity?* Was she really sent to release him? Where did she get her power from? So perfect. He watched her for a moment and touched the skylight as if he would reach through and touch her. He wondered what her skin felt like and longed to touch it. How soft would her hair be? How sweet would it smell? How warm and pure would her lips feel when they met his? The longing burned inside of him, but he knew he was forbidden . . . for now. *Enjoy this time,* he reminded himself. *The time between the wanting and the taking because it will be over before long.*

Chapter Nineteen

Grey was woken up by a thud, and then a horrible sound that had been all too familiar to her at one time. The morning sun streamed through the French doors as she sprung up in bed terrified! So many thoughts raced through her head in a split second before she jumped out of bed and ran down the hall. She ran into Mom's room and found her on the floor. Her body was heaving. Vomiting.

"Michael!" Grey screamed, running to Mom. Michael, half asleep, stumbled into the room. He stopped when he saw them on the floor.

"NO!" he screamed.

Grey was trying to be strong, but tears were flooding her eyes. Finally, Mom stopped vomiting, and her body went limp.

"Help me get her into bed."

Michael ran to them, and they lifted her into bed. Grey ran into Mom's bathroom and got a wet washcloth to wipe Mom's face.

"Mom, are you okay?" Grey asked, in a soft voice.

Mom nodded. Her eyes were closed. Grey reached for

her hand and felt her hot skin.

"Michael, get the thermometer."

Michael ran to the bathroom, taking the thermometer out of the medicine cabinet. He fumbled as he poured alcohol on a tissue and wiped it clean, running back into his mom's room.

"Mom, open your mouth. We're going to take your temperature," Grey said softly.

Mom opened her mouth slightly, and Michael put the thermometer under her tongue.

Grey and Michael sat silently. They nervously looked at each other. This couldn't happen again. When Dad got sick, they woke up to the same scene—Dad on the bedroom floor, vomiting. The only thing that was different was that Mom's body was on fire.

The thermometer beeped. Grey gently took it out of Mom's mouth. Ninety-eight point five.

"It's normal! That can't be right. You can feel the heat coming from her body." Grey handed the thermometer to Michael.

"Take it again."

Michael reset it, put it back in her mouth and again, they anxiously waited.

It beeped after a moment. Michael took it out this time, and again, ninety-eight point five.

"There must be something wrong with it. I'll go to the store and get another one."

"Okay," said Grey.

Michael ran out of the room.

"Hurry, Michael!" Grey turned to her mom. "Mom, are you okay?"

Slowly, Mom nodded.

Grey didn't like that Mom didn't seem strong enough to talk and was barely able to shake her head. She held onto Mom's hand.

In that moment, she realized how much Mom meant to her and what it would mean if she wasn't here anymore. She looked at Mom's face. It was very pale and was beginning to have the pallor of someone who is dying . . . losing blood flow. Haunting images of Dad at the end of his life overwhelmed her.

The tears streamed down her face. She couldn't lose her, she just couldn't.

"I love you, Mom. I need you. Please don't leave me. I'm sorry. I'm so sorry for everything."

She put her head on Mom's chest. Her heartbeat was faint. Grey realized that Mom must've suffered so much through Dad's illness, and she was so strong for them. She never felt the heaviness of this . . . of what Mom must've experienced. Mom protected she and Michael. She had taken Mom for granted and thought she was invincible, but she should have known better after the loss of Dad. She held onto Mom and cried.

Michael pedaled down the road as fast as he could. The store wasn't far at all, but he felt like he would never get there. His heart was beating through his chest. When the town came into view, he pedaled with all he had. He turned into the parking lot of the drugstore. Reaching the front door, he slammed on the brakes and dumped his bike on the ground. The flashbacks he was having about Dad were staggering. They engulfed him, making him lightheaded.

He ran into the store and down the aisles until he found the thermometers. There were so many! He scanned them quickly, grabbed one and ran to the counter. Fumbling with his money, he finally shoved all he had at the cashier and ran out without waiting for her to ring it up.

"Hey, your change!" she yelled after him.

He picked up his bike and jumped on it. He put his foot on the pedal—

"Michael!" He heard a familiar voice.

He turned around and saw Breel at the wheel of his pickup truck.

"I have to go!" Michael said.

"Wait, wait, are you okay?"

"No, it's my mom! Something's wrong."

"Let me drive you," Breel said.

Michael jumped off his bike and put it in the back of Breel's truck. He quickly opened the door, and Breel grabbed Michael by the arm, pulling him in as he hit the gas before he had a chance to close the door.

The truck raced down the road as Michael explained what had happened. Before he could finish the story, the pickup truck screeched into the driveway, and Michael jumped out, running up the steps, followed by Breel.

Michael burst into the house.

"Oh my God," he said out loud.

He was immediately enveloped with heat. It was so stifling that he stopped for a moment before running up the steps and down the hallway to Mom's room, Breel on his heels. When he ran into the room, Grey was sitting on the floor with her head on the bed, holding Mom's hand. She lifted her head and turned to face Michael, her face tear streaked. He tore the thermometer out of the wrapping, wiped it clean with alcohol and handed it to Grey.

"Mom, can you open your mouth?"

Mom didn't respond.

"Mom?"

Michael knelt on the floor next to the bed. "Mom?" he whispered. He shook her lightly. She didn't move.

"Mom!" Grey shouted as she tried in vain to get the thermometer in Mom's mouth. "Michael, what's wrong with her?!" she looked at him, tears streaming down her face. "Michael! This can't be happening!"

"911!" Michael said, reaching for his phone.

"I got this, stay with her," Breel said, grabbing the phone, and walking out of the room.

Michael wiped Mom's forehead with the washcloth.

Breel went down the hall where the Surge stood before him.

"What is going on?" Murial asked.

"Something is very wrong with Mrs. Masser, and I suspect it can't be helped by a doctor. She is burning up but doesn't have a fever. You can feel the heat in the house. The classic sign that it is celestial. She is very sick. We need to reverse it and fast."

"They've already been through so much," Neema said, sadly.

"We need to find Zale immediately. I am inclined to think he doesn't know anything about this. In the meantime, Micah will slow down the progression, or she will die."

"I've got this," Micah said, running down the hall, followed by Breel, Neema, and Murial.

Micah ran into the room. "My dad's a doctor. He's on his way," Micah said to Grey and Michael. He went over to her and quickly ran his hand across their mother's forehead while the rest of the Surge stood at the foot of the bed.

She slowly opened her eyes, and a small smile came across her lips when she saw her children kneeling next to the bed. "What's the matter?" she asked softly, looking around her room.

"Mom?" Grey whispered.

Mom pushed herself up, leaning against the headboard.

"Are you okay, Mom?" Michael asked.

"I'm fine," she said.

Grey and Michael looked at each other confused.

"Who's this?" Mom asked, gesturing to Micah.

"Oh . . . this is our friend, Micah," Michael said, still reeling from what had happened.

"Another friend I didn't know you had," Mom joked. "I'm Mrs. Masser."

"Well, you're meeting him now," Michael replied sheepishly.

"It's nice to meet you, Mrs. Masser," Micah replied.

Mom smiled and looked beyond Micah to the rest of the Surge.

". . . and they are?"

"Oh, that's Breel, Neema, and Murial."

"More friends."

They laughed.

Chapter Twenty

Breel paced in the middle of the Crest. He had to choose his words carefully and be strategic. He had to convince Zale that he needed Minna to reverse what she had done. This was an urgent, yet delicate, situation. He was very aware of the history Zale and Minna shared and how tight their bond had been over the centuries.

"What now?" Zale asked, with slight annoyance in his voice.

Breel turned around to find Zale leaning against the trunk of a white-barked tree. He cautiously walked toward him.

"I've been meaning to ask, how is the Mentor?"

Zale glanced at Breel. "I know we are not here for you to ask me that question."

Breel raised his eyebrows, waiting for an answer.

After a moment, Zale let out a sigh and looked directly at Breel. "I'm sure he is fine, doing what he does best, as always. You are boring me, Breel."

"Have you seen Minna?"

"Why?"

Breel hesitated for a moment.

"How many souls do you lose, and do we gain, if an Innocent is taken?"

"Is this about Grey because she touched the book? How many times do I have to remind you? She's my freedom and all," Zale replied, bored, waving his hands in the air.

"This is not about Grey."

"She is mine," Zale warned.

"How many souls?"

"You know how many."

"One thousand."

Zale looked at Breel. "Where are you going with this?"

"And how do you think the Mentor would feel if he lost one thousand souls?"

"Are you going to tell me what this is all about?"

"I would think he would be furious and show no mercy."

"Stop wasting my time!"

Breel didn't want to make him too angry. He was hoping to get Zale to a point where he would think seriously about what was happening and the repercussions. He would not want to have to tell the Mentor he was losing one thousand souls simply because Minna was angry and wanted revenge.

"Are you aware Minna is trying to take the life of an Innocent?"

Zale stared at Breel. The first person he instantly thought of was Grey.

"What do you mean?" he asked, concerned.

"She is trying to destroy Mrs. Masser, and you won't even get her soul. We will, because she is truly an Innocent and the

Mentor will have to forfeit one thousand souls."

"You are mad!" he snickered, walking toward him.

"Minna visited her three days ago. Mrs. Masser got very sick, and it wasn't something a doctor would be able to cure."

Zale stopped. He turned away from Breel, his smile fading, doubt filling his eyes. "Is this one of your subversions?" he asked, resting his hand on a tree.

"Minna paid Mrs. Masser a visit . . . Before she left, she hugged her."

Smoke rose from his hand on the tree. He knew Minna was upset with him, but to go this far? He slowly let his hand fall from the tree, revealing a handprint burnt into the tree.

"Micah had to stop it, but we both know that will not last long. Minna needs to reverse it," Breel ventured.

Zale didn't say anything.

". . . or you can."

Zale was silent.

"She will die . . . and you will have to explain to the Mentor why he has lost one thousand souls simply because Minna wanted revenge."

The ground beneath Zale began to smolder, smoke slowly rising. "How do I know you are not lying?" he asked.

"Really, Zale?"

Zale knew Breel wasn't lying. He just didn't want to give him satisfaction. There was no way to explain to the Mentor that he was about to lose one thousand souls for no reason except that Minna was, basically, pissed at Zale.

"Why don't you ask Minna yourself?"

"I will think about this." Zale walked away.

"There isn't time, Zale!"

Zale disappeared into the woods. As he walked through the dense foliage, paths cleared seamlessly for him in the direction he went, the ground left smoldering where he stepped. *How could a human, what he despises most, be the key to his freedom?* he wondered. Finally, a human he doesn't have disdain for, a human he admires, and yet, he needs to destroy. This was a punishment worse than his curse.

When Zale came out of the forest and onto the beach, it was dusk. He found Minna sitting on a rock on the deserted beach. She was facing the ocean with her long legs out in front of her, leaning back on her hands. Her long hair tumbling around her in the gentle breeze. He was reminded why he had loved her for so long. Aside from being beautiful, there was innocence to her appearance, a gracefulness to the way she moved. Yet, he knew she was capable of the evilest deeds.

Minna turned her head and watched Zale walk toward her. Zale jumped up on the rock and sat next to her. "Minna, we have a little problem."

"I love problems." She looked out over the ocean.

"You're not going to love this one."

"Try me."

"What happened with Grey's mom?"

"I don't know, what happened?"

Zale glanced at her, annoyed.

Minna smiled. "I was just having some fun."

There was no response from Zale.

"Oh, come on, this never bothered you before."

"She is an Innocent."

"Are you kidding me? I thought I was doing her a favor! She will be suffering more after the death of her daughter," she replied flatly, turning to look at him in the eye.

Zale scraped his nails along the rock he was sitting on, turning it into dust. Normally her response wouldn't bother him, but this time it did.

"What's the matter?"

He knew Minna could be dangerous. After all, she learned from him. A moment went by. They both looked out over the ocean. Zale dreaded what he had to say next. "You have to reverse it."

"Why?" A smile spread across her lips.

"Because I'm asking you to."

Minna laughed.

"And did you forget, if we take an Innocent, we have to give up one thousand souls."

"So?"

"That means in the end, the Surge wins. They get one thousand souls. Are you willing to allow that?"

Minna didn't answer.

"I think it's foolish to forfeit one thousand souls because you're angry with me. You are not only affecting me, but you are also affecting all the Fallen. You will make many enemies among us if you move forward with what you have done." Zale hoped she would see reason.

"So, we are evil, aren't we?"

"Yes, we are evil. But what you are doing does not make sense. It is defeating the purpose of what we do, and are you prepared to explain that to the Mentor?"

Minna thought about it for a moment. "This one might be worth it." She stood up, jumping off the rock.

Zale turned away angrily. He had to stay calm. He closed his eyes and took a deep breath.

"Minna, in all the centuries I have known you, you have never done anything like this. You have never done anything so reckless. You are smarter than this."

"I could say the same for you, Zale," she replied, keeping her voice light.

"What are you talking about?"

"Do you really want to have that conversation and if you did, would you be honest? I don't know if you've been honest with me lately and that hurts."

She was right. He wasn't being honest with her. He couldn't be. He wasn't even being honest with himself. He stood up on the rock and put his hands in his front pockets. He looked out over the vast ocean. The tide was coming in and the waves were gaining strength, angrily crashing on the beach.

"Don't make me reverse it."

Minna glared fiercely at Zale. "You wouldn't dare," she challenged.

Zale jumped off the rock and walked closer to her. "I would, Minna. I will not forfeit one thousand souls for one Innocent."

"Why, is it because it's Grey's mom?"

"Because it's not worth it."

"Maybe it is to me," Minna warned.

"There is nothing to gain."

"For me there is."

"What?"

She stepped closer to him, looking at him for a moment. He didn't flinch. "Satisfaction," she replied, smiling.

Zale clenched his hands at his sides, trying to stay calm. He was being forced to reluctantly play this game with her. "Minna, please! I have come to you first because we have a history. Please do not make me undo this. It will not make you look good. It will crack the foundation of your credibility."

"I can't believe you won't stand with me on this."

"No."

"What is happening to you? You are becoming weak. In the past you would have reveled in this. What has changed you?"

"Do not question me, Minna."

She began to walk down the beach. "Reverse it if you want. I don't care."

"What has this human done that you want to destroy her?" he yelled after her.

She turned and looked at Zale. "She had Grey," she said, seething.

Chapter Twenty-One

Grey and Michael sat on the couch in the living room. She was exhausted after the emotional day they had with Mom. She knew Michael was just as drained, especially when they found out Mom had no recollection of what happened. When they told her, she looked at them like they were crazy.

"I'm going to bed," Mom announced, walking into the living room.

"Good night, Mom," Grey and Michael said in unison.

Michael stood up, walked to Mom, and hugged her. She looked down at her hands and didn't move as Mom started to walk out of the living room. Grey quickly stood up. "Mom?"

Mom turned around.

Grey walked over and hugged her. She felt Mom hesitate for a moment before wrapping her arms around her and holding on tight.

"I love you, Mom."

Tears welled up in Mom's eyes. "I love you too, Grey." Mom's hug strengthened around Grey.

Michael watched from the couch and smiled.

"I'm so sorry, Mom." She cried, her arms tightening around Mom. Mom meant so much to her. Grey was grateful to be able to hold her.

"You don't have anything to be sorry about, Grey," Mom said, holding back the tears.

"I do, Mom. I've been pretty horrible."

"Oh, Grey. It's okay. You've been through a lot."

Grey and Mom slowly pulled away. Mom wiped her tears with her hand. "Please don't cry. We've all done enough of that."

"Thank you, Mom," Grey said softly.

"Thank you for what?"

"For everything . . . for this," she said as she looked around the living room.

"Aww, I just want you and Michael to be happy."

Grey smiled at Mom.

"I love you . . . and you, too." Mom's gaze landed on Michael.

"Mom, are you sure you're okay?" Grey asked.

"I'm fine. Don't worry." Mom held Grey's face in her hands.

Grey nodded.

"We're going to get through this. I promise."

Grey nodded again.

Michael went to Mom and hugged her. "Love you, Mom," said Michael.

Mom smiled. "Okay, enough of this. I'm going to bed."

"Good night, Mom," Grey said.

Grey and Michael watched Mom walk down the hallway.

They sat on the couch. Michael turned his head and smiled at her.

"So, what happened?"

"What do you mean?"

"All of the sudden you care about Mom."

"I've always cared about Mom."

"Grey, you're talking to your brother here."

She looked down. "Michael, I wanted to say so much more, but I couldn't get the words out."

Michael was silent.

"I wanted to thank her for being my mom. I wanted to thank her for always being there for me. I know she's trying to give us a great summer, to keep us together as a family."

Michael hesitated a moment. "Grey, what happened that you've all of a sudden came to this epiphany?"

"Epiphany? Since when do you use the word 'epiphany'?"

"Since now."

She hesitated and looked down at her hands. "I've been realizing things."

"What kind of things?"

"I don't know. Since we've been here, things are changing. The way I feel is changing. It's weird." She shrugged her shoulders, looking at her brother. "I just didn't realize Mom might be going through the same things as me . . . as us." She gestured toward Michael.

Michael smiled at her.

"What?"

"I'm proud of you, Grey."

She looked down at her hands and didn't say anything.

"Hey, what's the matter?" asked Michael.

"I'm worried about Mom."

"Me too."

"She won't see a doctor."

"Because she has no recollection of what happened, and she feels fine now."

"I can't believe that after everything we've been through with Dad, she won't see a doctor . . . for us."

"I know."

"I'm scared, Michael."

"Me too." Michael sighed.

"Today I realized what a terrible person I've been . . . and selfish."

"I'm not going to argue with you on that one."

"Thanks."

"You're welcome."

Grey looked away. "It took me thinking we were going to lose Mom to realize this. What is wrong with me?"

"You pushed us away."

"I was so scared and confused and, and just lost . . ." Tears filled her eyes.

"I know, Grey, but that's not how you deal with things. You don't shut people out, especially your family, considering we're all you have."

"If anything ever happened to Mom, I don't know what I would do."

Michael didn't say anything.

"Michael?"

Michael looked at his sister. "I know."

"What happens when she dies?" she asked slowly, tears rolling down her face.

Michael grabbed her hand. "I hope that we won't have to worry about that for a long time."

The sun was high as Grey and Michael turned onto the main street in town. Long, streaky clouds slowly floated along, crossing over the sun at times, casting a dark shadow below every now and then. It was still early enough that most of the stores weren't open yet, except for a couple of restaurants that served breakfast.

Michael looked over at his sister. "I'm proud of you Grey."

Grey smiled as she looked straight ahead. "I know, you told me that last night."

"Well, I'm telling you again. And you know how happy you made Mom, right?"

Grey took a deep breath as her throat tightened and her eyes glazed over. She looked at Michael and could only nod as she held back the tears. *Why had she waited so long?*

"So, what's on the list?"

"What list?"

"The grocery list."

"I don't know. I don't have it."

"Yes, you do. I gave it to you."

"No, you didn't."

Michael leaned back on his bike seat. "I don't have any pockets. See, bathing suit. No pockets."

Grey furrowed her brow and put her hand in her right

front pocket steadying her bike. Nothing. She reached into her left pocket. Something crumpled up at the very bottom brushed her fingertips. She reached in a little deeper and pulled out the list.

"See, I told you," said Michael.

Just then, a gust of wind blew the list out of Grey's hand. "Oh no!"

Startled, Grey and Michael watched it for a moment, then raced after it. The wind carried it down the street before it fluttered in the air, disappearing down a side street.

They quickly followed it, turning down the street, the paper tumbling along the cobblestones. About halfway down the block, on the right side of the street, it floated up steps and came to a stop against a door.

They stopped in front of the steps. Grey got off her bike and quickly lowered it to the ground. She ran up the steps and grabbed the small piece of paper before it could be blown away again. Turning to walk down the steps, she noticed how unusual the street was. She hadn't paid much attention because she was focused on the small piece of paper.

It was quiet, like time was standing still. The street was about half the length of the other streets on the key and much narrower. It was lined with small dark stone buildings along both sides that all had the same wooden lattice windows with peeling paint here and there. Steps were crumbling and the buildings themselves appeared to be in disrepair. They all seemed abandoned, except for the store in front of Grey.

Grey looked at Michael. "What is this?"

He looked down the desolate street. "It's weird, that's

what it is."

"It's like we stepped back in time."

Grey turned around and looked at the small store. Vines with heart-shaped leaves crawled up one side of the building. Books stacked carelessly on the windowsill inside, teetering on top of one another. It looked dark inside except for a yellow glow that emanated from somewhere in the store. A worn black sign with burnished gold script read Happy Wanderer Bookstore hung from the building on a black iron rod.

Grey stuffed the list in her front pocket. "It's a bookstore. Let's go in," she muttered.

"Really?"

"I love bookstores." Grey marched up the steps.

Michael rolled his eyes. "I know." Michael took a deep breath before getting off his bike and laying it next to hers. He trudged up the steps as she turned the black iron doorknob. Michael grabbed the door above her and held it open.

They stepped in, immediately hit with a musty book smell. It wasn't as dark as it appeared from outside. The door shut. Dust swirled around in the glow of yellow light.

The stores walls were lined with old, dark wooden bookcases from floor to ceiling, filled with books. In the middle of the store were two smaller bookshelves back-to-back engulfed in books. To their immediate left was an old-fashioned cash register with metal keys on a small dark wooden counter. The place seemed vacant.

Grey walked deeper into the store, leaving Michael standing by himself as he looked around, his mouth half open. She wandered down the aisle, looking at the shelves of books which were bound in leather and covered in a thick layer of dust. *Didn't anyone ever shop here?*

"Grey." Michael called out. She looked up. The books on top of the bookshelf moved apart as Michael peeked his head through. "Do you think anyone is here?"

"I don't know."

"Come here and look at this."

Grey walked around to Michael. The bookshelf had a glass front with a lock on it. Michael tugged on the old lock, and it opened. He looked at Grey and smiled before unhooking the lock and opening the glass.

"Michael—" Grey began to protest.

"Look, these books are old. Really old." he said taking a book from the shelf. He opened the cover slowly. "This is a first edition."

"That's crazy."

He put the book back and took another one. "This one too. "Do you know how rare these are?"

"All the books seem so old," she said, looking around.

"I saw some newer ones over there." He pointed behind him as he went around to the other side.

Grey turned around and looked at the books. She saw Dickens, Thomas Wolfe, Dylan Thomas, Fitzgerald, Austen. *This wasn't your average bookstore that you'd find back home.* She continued to walk to the front of the store and stopped to peruse the books that were stacked on the windowsill. As she went through them, she was not paying attention to how high she was piling them. She placed one on top of the precariously piled books and they all came crashing down. She tried in vain to stop them from falling but was overtaken by the number of books. She quickly knelt to pick them up.

Michael came running over and knelt next to her. "What happened?"

"I think you know what happened," said Grey.

Together they quickly tried to put the books back on the windowsill. Grey stopped. A small smile came across her lips and her eyes welled up with tears as she picked up one of the books. She ran her fingers across the front of the book.

Michael nudged her. "What are you doing?"

She didn't move. She held the book out to him, and when he saw the title, he stopped. He reached out to take it from her. He looked at it for a moment and hugged his sister.

Behind them, they heard creaking floorboards under short, quickened footsteps.

"Oh, don't worry about those. I'll take care of them later," a voice said.

Grey and Michael, still sitting on the floor, turned around. A little bespectacled man put a pen in the pocket of his white button-down shirt. He chuckled as he walked toward them, straightening his bow tie.

Michael began putting the books back, quickening his pace, as the man extended his hand to Grey.

"Here, let me help you, young lady."

Grey gently took his hand. "I'm sorry. I was looking at the books and I knocked everything over."

The man waved his hand. "Oh, don't worry about it. It was a teetering mess. They all have to go."

"You're getting rid of them?"

The man gave her an amused look. "Yes, yes. So, help yourselves, please."

Grey held the book close to her chest. "Thank you."

"What do you have there?" He smiled, rubbing his hands together.

She held the book out to the man.

"Ah, yes. *The Little Prince.* A fine book, but it doesn't sell around here. These people have no taste."

Grey smiled.

Michael put the last of the books on the windowsill, brushed himself off, and stood up. The man looked Michael up and down, folded his arms, and squinted a little before walking behind the counter.

"You wouldn't want a job, would you?"

Michael put his hand to his chest. "Me?"

The man chuckled again. "Yes, I need someone around here who is strong and takes the initiative to do things. You seem like that kind of person by the way you picked up all those books."

"Sure! But I'm only here for the summer."

"I'll take it! I pay fifteen dollars an hour. I could use you for about twenty hours a week."

The man extended his hand. "I may only be around here for the summer too," he said, joking.

Michael accepted his handshake.

The man stuffed his hands into the pockets of his black trousers. "Can you start tomorrow, ten o'clock?"

"Sure," Michael said with a big smile on his face. "Mr.—?"

The man smiled, scratching at nary a piece of hair on his

head. "Oliver, just Oliver."

"I'm Michael, and this is my sister, Grey."

Oliver nodded. "It's nice to meet you both."

She looked at Michael who took a deep breath.

"Well, you too, get out of here and enjoy the beautiful day." He dismissed them as he walked to the back of the store.

"Thank you!" Michael called after him before opening the door for Grey.

The door closed as Oliver reached the back of the store. He hesitated . . . turned around and craned his chubby neck, looking to make sure Grey and Michael were gone. A long shadow cast itself along the floor.

"Good job," a voice said behind him. A cloaked figure with piercing yellow eyes stepped toward Oliver.

"I thought so," he chuckled.

Chapter Twenty-Two

om is going to be so excited for you!" Grey climbed the last step to the house.

"I can't believe I got a job!" He quickly opened the door and they burst into the living room.

They walked into the kitchen carrying the grocery bags and found Mom standing at the counter making herself a cup of coffee.

"Hi, Mom," Michael said, putting the grocery bags on the counter.

"Michael has something to tell you," Grey announced, standing next to her brother.

Mom leaned on the counter with a spoon in her hand. "Look at you two grinning from ear to ear."

Neither one of them said anything.

"Well, are you going to tell me?"

"Michael got a job!" Grey blurted out.

Mom dropped the spoon on the floor, the smile quickly faded from her lips. Grey and Michael looked at each other, their smiles disappearing.

"Mom? I thought you would be happy for me."

"What?" She put her hands to her head and turned away. "No, Michael."

"Mom, he's trying to help." Grey walked to Mom, tilting her head in confusion. Grey saw Mom's eyes well up. She put her arm around Mom.

"I don't want you to work, Michael. I want you to enjoy your summer," Mom said, trying to fight back the tears.

"But I want to help."

She looked at her son. "I know you do, but it's not your responsibility."

"It kind of is, Mom."

She shook her head. "No, it isn't. It's my responsibility."

"It's at a cool bookstore. It'll be fun."

"He's really excited, Mom," Grey chimed in.

Mom looked at both of her children. "Come here." She hugged them. "I love you two so much. I just want you both to be happy."

Michael looked at Mom. "We are happy."

"I'm proud of you, Michael, but I don't want either of you to feel you have to work. Do you understand me?"

"Yes, Mom," they said, smiling.

Mom managed a smile and shook her head.

Grey sat cross-legged in her white nightgown on top of her bed, *The Little Prince* opened in front of her. She wiped the tears from her face and closed the book. She walked to the French doors and peeked out, looking up at the star-filled sky.

"Where are you, Dad? I miss you."

She lingered there for a few moments; then, she walked back to the bed and grabbed the book, clutching it to her chest as she left her room.

She stood in Michael's doorway, watching her brother as he sat in bed reading his book. Finally, he looked up at her. "What?"

"Nothing," she replied, walking in and sitting on his bed.

Michael quickly moved his legs so she wouldn't sit on them. "Make yourself comfortable."

"I will." She crossed her legs as she placed the book in her lap. "Michael, do you remember the part in *The Little Prince* about how you can only see with your heart because what is important you can't see with your eyes?"

Michael closed his book putting it on the bed. "I don't."

"I didn't realize the book was about life and love. We were so young. I didn't really get it all."

"Dad always picked good books, even if we didn't understand them at the time."

Grey hesitated. "Don't you think it's a little strange that we came across this book the way we did?"

Michael crossed his arms. "*We* didn't come across it, *you* did."

Grey shook her head. "I didn't see any other children's books at the store today. Did you?"

"No, I didn't, but it was in the 'free' pile, so maybe Oliver had a children's section at one time."

Grey wasn't convinced. "Really?"

"What?"

"I just think it's strange. That's all."

Michael stared at his sister.

Grey looked down. "What if . . . what if Dad is trying to send us a message?"

Michael put his book on the nightstand. "Go to bed, Grey."

"I'm serious. Look, he may have read this to us when we were little, and we may not remember much of it, but all of a sudden, it comes to us during a time when we need what this book talks about."

"Grey, I understand you miss Dad. I miss him too, but you're reaching."

"Michael, it's about how to navigate life. How to deal with people we might cross paths with. Having determination and hope."

"Grey—"

"I think it talks about love. Do you remember the part about the rose?"

Michael took a deep breath. He crossed his arms, shaking his head. "That little liar."

Grey smiled. "And the snake, do you remember the snake? I think it represented evil or death."

Michael shrugged. "I always thought it represented the devil."

Grey looked at Michael and tilted her head. She pushed the book toward him. "I'm leaving this here. You need to read it."

Michael sighed as she got up and walked out.

Grey didn't know that so many things in the book would mean so much to her. When she was little, it was just a book

Dad read to her. She didn't realize it was about life lessons, at least that's how she interpreted it now. She was too young then. Dad had left her with so many gifts. One thing he taught her was to look with her heart. That's what she was doing with Zale. She knew, despite what Michael might think, Zale was good. She felt it.

Chapter Twenty-Three

rey and Michael pedaled down the road. She didn't
want to leave Mom, but Mom insisted, telling them she
was fine and that there was no reason for them to stay home.
She felt guilty, and she knew Michael did as well.

She was beginning to think that Michael's idea of riding
their bikes to the party wasn't so great after all. The sun was
pretty high, though it was evening, and she was perspiring.
The last thing she wanted to do was show up all sweaty to
a party in front of beautiful people. She couldn't wait until
she got her license so she could drive, but until then, she was
stuck riding a bike. She was annoyed at the situation. While
she was really enjoying her time on Sleepy Key, she was still
disappointed that she wouldn't be able to take her driver's test
until September when they went back home. Michael didn't
seem to care at all. He was so happy to be here. He actually
never brought up the issue of not getting his driver's license on
his birthday. He always lived in the moment, rarely looking to
the future, and just rolled with whatever came his way.

Michael coasted, allowing Grey to catch up.

"Come on, slowpoke," he said.

"Michael, I don't want to be all sweaty when I get there," she complained as she cruised next to him.

Michael was preoccupied with something on his phone.

"Don't you care if you're sweaty?" she asked.

"No, why?" he asked, continuing to look at his phone.

"Did you even take a shower after work today?"

"Uhhh . . . no."

Grey shook her head. "Oh, Michael. Okay, where is this place?"

"That's what I'm trying to figure out. My navigation isn't working." They slowed down as they reached the end of the key. "The address is 4047."

"Well, we're at the end of the Key." Grey stopped, straddling her bike.

Michael stopped next to her. They looked around.

"Maybe we should go home. I'm worried about Mom." She pulled her phone out of her back pocket.

Michael raised his eyebrows. "You have your phone?"

"Yes, I have my phone, but I don't have service." She moved it around, trying to get signal. "I don't like that I can't reach Mom by phone. What if she needs us?"

"Grey, I would have never left her if she wasn't okay."

She nervously picked at the edge of her phone case.

"Grey, we won't stay long, okay."

"Alright." She looked around. "You don't think they gave us the wrong address on purpose, do you? Maybe there isn't a party."

"Grey, why would Breel do that? He started talking to

us, remember?" Michael reminded her. He turned around, looking back down the road.

"What?"

"Come on."

Passed the beach on their right, there was a small opening in the brush, just big enough for a small car to get through. Michael pedaled over to it and disappeared through the brush. Grey quickly pedaled to the opening. The last thing she wanted was to be left alone. The memory of what had happened to her with the snake was still fresh in her mind.

"Michael," she called out in a loud whisper.

"Come on, Grey. I think it's back here."

"Are you kidding?" she asked herself out loud. Grey ducked her head under the low hanging tree branches at the opening and pedaled until she saw Michael down the crushed seashell path. He waved for her to come to him. The farther down the path she went, the more open it became. "Is this it?" she asked.

"I think so. Look," he said, holding out his phone. "4047, right? Well, the last house we passed before the beach was 4045, and the house across the street was 4048. So, when I saw the opening, I figured maybe there was a house back here."

"Yeah, but where *is* the house?" Grey asked.

"I don't know. Let's go see." He lifted himself onto the bike seat and pedaled.

Everything was twisted and intertwined, causing it to be darker and more shadowy than on the road. The obscurity sent a chill through her. The trees and brush pushed back, the grounds opening up as she rode down what was becoming more of a driveway. The area began to change, like something beautiful coming to life. Darkness into light. Grey looked around at the flowering bushes with their big red and white flowers and the vines that hung down from the tall trees that danced in the gentle breeze.

They rode up a small hill. The seashell driveway turned into white marble. It split around a fountain shooting water into the air from the tops of an angel's outspread wings. Behind the fountain was a white marble structure that rose into the sky like a castle. It stood tall and strong and was weathered with age, but nevertheless, beautiful. There was something enchanting about it though the sheer scale made it slightly ominous.

Grey and Michael looked at each other.

"Where are we?" Grey finally asked.

"I don't know, but this is pretty cool," Michael said in awe.

"Cool? Okay, you can go with that. I was thinking more along the lines of strange, maybe even odd."

"I didn't ask you," he said, teasing her. "Come on."

He leaned his bike up against a tree. Grey placed her bike up against his. She turned around but didn't move. She wanted to move, but her feet felt like they were submersed in thick mud. Her brain was telling them to move, but they weren't going anywhere. She was suddenly overcome with uncertainty.

"What?" he asked.

"Maybe we should go home," she whispered.

"Are you crazy?"

"Michael, look at this house."

"What about it? And why are you whispering?" His

eyes narrowed.

"I don't know." She stared downward. "Maybe we don't belong here."

"What are you talking about?" Michael's brows arched upward. "We were invited."

"Hello!" someone called out in a cheery voice.

Grey turned around. The petite blonde woman from Regular's Coffee House poked her head out of the massive front door, which made her look tinier than she really was. For a fleeting moment, Grey wondered how she had opened the door by herself.

"Oh, hi," Michael said, recognition sparking in his eyes. He turned back to his sister. "Ha! We can't leave now."

Grey didn't have a choice at this point. She couldn't just get on her bike and pedal away. That would be ridiculous.

"Come on!" The woman waved her hand. "Everyone is out back."

It's now or never. Grey took a step forward. Her legs felt like rubber bands, and she wasn't sure if she would make it to the front door. Why did she get so nervous in situations like this? Michael turned around and grabbed her arm, pulling her along. "We've been waiting for you," the woman said to them. Before Grey could say anything, the petite blonde introduced herself. "I'm Lil."

"I'm Michael, and this is my sister, Grey."

"I know." Lil grinned.

Shadow, the little black dog from the coffee shop, ran to the edge of the steps to greet them. His little legs moved as if he were walking in place, and he wagged his tail around in a circle.

"Shadow!" Michael quickened his pace toward the dog. Grey hurried along with him. She really didn't have a choice, considering he was still pulling her. Michael bent down to pet the happy puppy who gently jumped up and licked his face.

"He really likes you." Lil laughed.

"He's such a cool dog," Michael replied.

Shadow ran over to Grey and stood on his hind legs trying to reach her, his front paws outstretched. Grey bent down on her knees and rubbed the dog behind his ears. He rolled over on his back and allowed Grey to rub his white belly.

"Come on in," Lil said.

Shadow jumped up and ran into the house. Grey and Michael followed as Lil held the door.

They stepped into the grand, white marble foyer of the house. There were two marble staircases, one to the right and one to the left, that went up the circular foyer to a balcony on the second level. The black banister was so shiny, and the intricate detail of the carving was something she had never seen before. Was the banister marble too? *It had to be.*

They followed Lil straight back through the house. There were smaller hallways off the main hallway, but they were so long, Grey couldn't see where they ended. Massive pieces of artwork hung on the walls, and although she wasn't up on her art, she had a feeling they were very old, expensive pieces.

Lil swung open a white floor to ceiling door, and they stepped into the kitchen, which had a white and black tile floor and old-fashioned appliances. *What an odd combination.* She could tell Michael hadn't picked up on any of this because he was too busy talking to Lil. It amazed Grey how her brother could just strike up a conversation with anyone at any time. It didn't matter who they were or where they were.

"How is your mom doing?" Lil asked.

"She's much better," said Michael.

"Good, I'm glad. Things like that can be so scary."

"We weren't sure if we should come tonight and leave her, but she insisted she was okay."

Grey had her head down. She really felt guilty for leaving Mom home alone.

"Are you okay?" asked Lil.

"I'm still worried about her," Grey said, quietly.

"Of course, you are. It was quite a scare from what Breel told me."

Grey could see everyone out on the deck through the windows, which spanned the back wall of the kitchen. She panicked a little. She had to make sure Michael didn't leave her alone. She could hear the music playing faintly. It was instrumental, yet a little dark. *Maybe they listen to different music here.* She scanned the partygoers. Was there anyone she recognized? She saw the girls who were with Breel at Regular's, and as she continued to scan, she saw Breel. He was laughing at something that was said, pushing his hair out of his face. It was nice to be able to watch people without them knowing. She felt safe doing this, much safer than talking to people face to face.

"Grey?" Lil called out.

As she turned to look at her, someone caught her eye out on the deck. She stiffened. It was Minna, who was staring at her through the window.

"What can I get you?" Lil asked.

Minna gave her a quick, hard smile.

Grey looked back at Lil. "Oh, I'm fine right now. Thank you." She tried to get her bearings and calm herself down. If she was there, then Zale must already be here, too.

Chapter Twenty-Four

Grey and Michael stepped out onto the deck. The music was much louder than she thought it would be. She immediately felt Minna's cold stare. She glanced to her right and saw Minna's gaze locked on her.

"Don't leave me," she whispered to Michael.

"Don't worry, I won't."

Grey followed as Michael walked to the edge of the deck. The branches of the tall trees hung over the deck in some places, creating little alcoves allowing one to hide if they chose. The house was on the edge of a peninsula. They watched the waves crash on the beach and return to the ocean with rhythmic grace.

The deck was made of a white stone with a railing that disappeared around the house in both directions. Grey wanted to follow the deck and explore, but she wouldn't dare leave Michael's side. The sun was just dipping below the waterline, allowing the faint outline of the stars against the darkening sky to appear.

"Okay, Grey, I have to go to the bathroom."

"We just got here!" She stomped her foot.

"I know, but I have to go."

"You've got to be kidding me!"

"Believe me, I'm not."

"You can't."

"Now you've got to be kidding me. I have to go."

"You told me you wouldn't leave me. I'll come with you."

"No, you're not."

"Hey, you two. I'm glad you made it." Breel walked toward them.

"Hey Breel. Thanks for inviting us," replied Michael.

Grey smiled at Breel. "Thank you."

"We almost didn't find it. It's a little hidden."

"Oh, I'm sorry about that. I should have told you. Everything is so concealed around here and so overgrown. I guess I'm just used to it and don't think about it."

"No problem. We made it," said Michael.

"We're glad you did," said Neema, smiling at them.

"Hey, you remember Neema, Micah, and Murial."

"Yeah. Hi," replied Michael.

"Hi," Grey said, stepping slightly behind her brother.

"This is really some house. How long have you lived here?" Michael asked, looking up at the house.

There he goes. Asking the questions he probably shouldn't be asking so soon, or at least asking the questions she would never have the nerve to ask.

"Oh, we've lived here for a long time." Breel shrugged.

"It must've been one of the first built on the key," said Michael.

"Yes. I think it was," replied Breel. "We'll show you around later."

"That would be great. Do you think in the meantime you could show me where the bathroom is?" asked Michael.

Grey couldn't believe he snuck it in there like that. He totally caught her off guard.

"Sure, come on."

"I'll be right back," Michael told Grey.

Grey widened her eyes at her brother, but he ignored her.

"She'll be fine," assured Murial.

He told her he wouldn't leave her and there he went, leaving her. She watched Michael and Breel disappear into the house.

"I know you," a voice drawled.

She turned around. Minna stood behind Murial, Neema, and Micah who didn't budge to make room for her. *They must be blocking Minna on purpose.*

"Well, aren't you going to say 'Hi'?" Minna asked sarcastically.

"Hi," Grey said hesitantly.

"You know Minna?" asked Neema.

"We've met." Grey averted her eyes from Minna.

She wished her brother was back. While Minna hadn't said much, Grey knew by the tone of her voice that she didn't like her and wasn't going to be nice. She stood there, looking down at her with a smirk on her face, her feet apart, hip thrust to one side, and her head held high. It made her very uncomfortable.

"How's your mom doing?" she asked with a smile.

Neema threw her a dirty look.

Grey hesitated. *How did she know?* "She's fine."

"Yeah, I heard she was *very* sick."

"Enough, Minna," said Micah.

Minna threw her head back and laughed. Her smile vanished. "By the way, Zale's not here, and I don't know how long you'll be here either," Minna said in a cold tone.

"Minna!" Murial warned.

"What? I was just letting the poor thing know," Minna replied with fake sympathy. "We all know how Zale can be. Have fun while you can." She leered.

Grey was stunned. How did she know about them? Her heart sank. Why didn't this girl like her? She didn't even know her!

Minna was distracted, looking past Grey, who was grateful for the reprieve. "Who's that?" asked Minna seductively, as she began to slowly walk away.

Grey turned around. Michael and Breel walked toward them.

"No one you would be interested in," said Murial.

"That's what you think," Minna said, not taking her eyes off Michael.

"You're cute," Minna cooed as Michael approached.

Michael was caught off guard. "What?"

Minna lightly brushed Michael with her body as she slowly walked past him. "We need to talk," she continued.

"Not now," Breel said, voice harsh.

"Later, then," Minna said to Michael, unfazed by Breel's words as she walked away.

"She is no one you would or should be interested in," Breel replied.

"Bad news," agreed Micah.

Grey looked at Michael, trying to get his attention without anyone noticing. She didn't want him to leave her again.

"Don't let her bother you," Micah said to Grey. "She's pretty obnoxious to everyone."

"So, it's not just me?" Grey asked, half kidding.

"Oh, no," said Neema.

"Well, that's good to know," Grey said with a smile, trying to shake off what just happened.

They all laughed.

"Isn't that the girl who drives the red convertible?" Michael whispered to Grey.

"Yes. Stay away from her," she whispered to her brother.

"Hey, let's go over here," Breel said, gesturing to a table at the edge of the deck.

They sat at the table overlooking the ocean. Grey was still concerned about Mom, but she was beginning to relax. Everyone was nice to her, and she hadn't seen Minna around. Zale hadn't showed up, but it was still early. The faint outline of the soon-to-be Copper Moon lit the dim sky. She looked up at it. Would she see her first Copper Moon without Zale?

A group of kids walked out onto the deck from the kitchen. Grey tried to be as nonchalant as possible as she scanned the group for Zale.

"Don't worry, I'm sure he'll be here," Michael said.

How did he know that she was looking for him? Maybe she wasn't being so nonchalant after all. "I need to go to the bathroom," Grey told him.

"It's in through the kitchen, to the right, and down the steps."

Grey walked through the interesting crowd and wondered where they all came from. They seemed so cool the way they dressed. No one looked at her weird because she wore plain black cutoff jeans and a T-shirt. If she were back home, she would be subjected to unpleasant stares if she wasn't dressed a certain way, but she never let this bother her. Her parents always taught her to be an individual and not to worry about what others thought, so she was used to tuning people out though she longed to fit in sometimes. She felt somewhat comfortable here, and that allowed her to be a little braver.

She opened the door and stepped into the empty kitchen, closing the door behind her. She walked around the island in the middle of the kitchen to an archway on the right with steps that led down into eventual darkness. She looked for a light switch but couldn't find one. She could go back outside and ask someone, but she really had to use the bathroom.

She looked down the steps and figured she could make it down without hurting herself because the light from the kitchen illuminated the staircase slightly. Once she got down there, she could feel around for a light switch. She slowly went down the steps, the light from the kitchen fading. The wall to the left was made of glass blocks, and the lights outside shone through the glass, making distorted shapes on the opposite wall. They looked like tiny dancing spirits, and that's all she needed for her imagination to go wild. She froze, having second thoughts about continuing down the steps. She kept her head turned to the left, looking at the wall with the glass blocks and avoiding the wall with the dancing spirits.

The air suddenly grew cold. She wanted to go back, but she was a little stuck, afraid to go down, yet afraid to go up. She took a deep breath and forced herself to go down one more step cautiously, and then another, and another into the darkness, all the while feeling around with her feet and holding onto the walls with her outstretched arms. She took the last step on solid ground. She slowly fumbled around on the walls for the light switch. Nothing.

She was in total darkness. She groped around again, quicker this time, running her hands along the rough wall, which felt like cement, and again, nothing! Her heart was beating faster and faster. *What should I do?* She felt something that made her go numb. What was it? If she didn't know any better, she would swear it was an icy cold breath as if someone were standing inches from her face. Her heart continued to beat faster, pounding in her ears. Who, or what, was breathing on her, and why was it so cold? She was frozen, screaming inside. Something hissed. Grey felt things slithering up her bare legs. *What was it? Snakes!* Just as she was about to scream, she heard menacing laughter all around her. She opened her mouth to scream but nothing came out.

"Grey, are you down there?" a voice called as the light switched on.

"Yes!" Grey screeched. She opened her eyes and looked around frantically. There wasn't anyone or anything there. She looked up the stairway and saw Lil standing at the top of the steps.

"Oh, you poor dear. You went down there in the dark?"

"I couldn't find the switch," she said, trying to calm herself. "I thought it might be down here."

"It's this cord hanging from the ceiling."

"Oh, I didn't see it." Grey's face reddened.

"No one sees it," Lil replied, sympathetically. "We really need to put a wall switch in. This house is so old."

How could she not see the cord hanging from the ceiling? *How am I so stupid?* Grey went into the bathroom, switched the light on, and locked the door behind her. She leaned on the bathroom door, taking a deep breath before sliding down the door. She sat on the cold black-and-white tile floor, pulling her knees to her chest, curling herself up into a tight ball. Her throat ached as she choked back the tears. *Where was Dad?* Tears rolled down her face. She needed him. She needed him to hold her, and whenever she got scared, she looked for him. She stayed on the floor a few minutes. Reaching for a tissue, she wiped the tears from her face.

Chapter Twenty-Five

G rey didn't want to go back upstairs. She knew she looked like she had been crying and didn't want anyone to see her. She slowly opened the door, making sure that no one else was waiting. She walked out of the bathroom. A door to the left seemed to lead outside. She turned the knob slowly, not wanting to make any noise in case Lil was still upstairs and stepped out into the night. She leaned against the house and took another deep breath as she thought about getting on her bike and going home. But leaving wouldn't be fair to Michael. He would worry about her and wonder where she went.

She followed the slate path that led to the front of the house. Voices made her stop. She stepped back into the bushes. She briefly thought about how ridiculous it was that she was hiding in the bushes. A group of kids walked down the path along the side of the house to the party. She stepped out and continued down the path, turning into an opening to her left that was dimly lit. There were tiny white lights strung throughout the trees and an old, weathered cement bench. She sat down and tried to calm herself, trying to figure out what had happened in the darkness. She was sure some-one lurked down there with her. She didn't imagine the cold breath on her face, and she heard the laughter. It was a girl's laugh. Very sinister. The thought of it sent chills down her spine. She tried to compose herself and looked up at the trees that formed a protective cocoon around her.

"Grey," a familiar voice said.

She lowered her head to find Zale standing in front of her. His long, lean body was defined by his tight black T-shirt and black jeans. His dark hair hung in his face. The reflection from the lights in the trees appeared to make his body glow all over.

"Hi." Grey's heart fluttered. *Where did he come from?* She never heard him coming or going.

"I was looking for you," he said, cocking his head to one side, causing his hair to almost cover half of his face.

"Oh," she said, trying to be cool. He was looking for her?

"Once again, I find you alone."

Grey lowered her gaze and smiled.

"Why aren't you with everyone else?" he asked.

"I was, but I wanted to get away for a while."

"Yeah, these parties can be a little dull." He walked over, sitting next to her.

Grey dug her fingertips into the cement bench. "You've been here before?" she asked.

"Yeah."

"I thought you didn't know them."

"What?"

"You told me you didn't know them that day at the

drum circle."

"I would prefer *not* to know them." He leaned forward, resting his elbows on his knees, and clasped his hands together.

"Why did you come then?"

Zale looked down at the ground for a moment. "I came for you." He looked at her. "The One."

A chill ran through her body. Grey didn't know what to say. There was silence between them. She didn't even hear the music playing any longer. She was lost in what Zale had just said.

"I want to show you something," he said, holding her gaze. He stood up. "Will you come with me?"

Grey nodded. Zale gently reached for her hand and took it. Her heart skipped a beat. His hand was warm, and her hand felt comfortable in his. He led her out of the opening and down the slate path to the front of the house where he crossed into the woods. He stepped to the side to part the branches that blocked their way and smiled at her as he brushed past her. She followed Zale down a labyrinth of wooded paths through the thick green brush that was only lit by the Copper Moon. She didn't know where they were going. That was fine with her. The fact that she left Michael back at the party didn't even cross her mind after making it very clear to Michael not to leave her.

She felt like this was a big adventure and she was okay with it. She wasn't afraid. There was something different about Zale, almost like he wasn't real. He wasn't anything like the other boys back home.

She watched Zale walking in front of her as he held her

hand. The moonlight allowed her to catch glimpses of him without him noticing.

They reached an area blocked by dense, twisted foliage. Zale turned around, gaze locked on hers before he reached out with his hand and effortlessly moved the branches aside for her to walk through. This time, her body lightly brushed his as she walked past him. Her breath caught.

Grey ducked as she stepped through, and when she looked up, she saw a fantastical wonderland. She didn't move. She couldn't believe what she was seeing.

Zale took a few steps closer to her and whispered in her ear, "Go ahead. It's for you . . . all of its wonderful beauty."

Grey took a few steps in and looked around, bewildered. The trees seemed to sparkle. As she looked closer, she saw tiny black lanterns whose flames shimmered along the twisted branches of the trees. As she continued down the path, she encountered black butterflies that fluttered freely in the air. Small, worn stone benches tucked away along the path seemed as if they had grown from the earth. She felt like she was in a fairy tale.

Grey turned back and looked for Zale, but he wasn't there. She quickly turned back around to find him in front of her with his hands in the pockets, smiling at her. He sauntered back a step, his eyes shining with a silent invitation for her to follow.

Grey followed Zale. The mystical trees and foliage parted. He stepped aside, revealing a large black marble structure ascending into the sky that looked like it was from another world. Time had worn the marble away, revealing swirls of gray, and the black paint peeled away from the trim of the large windows. There were immense black wrought iron gates that guarded the front door, and while it was very beautiful, something was very sinister about it. She stood with her eyes wide, her mouth agape, and she caught herself.

Zale stood on the steps watching her. He pulled open the heavy gates for her with ease, though a high-pitched scraping noise escaped, and Grey walked toward him.

As she got closer, she could see that the wrought iron was twisted into shapes of little creatures with contorted expressions. Their faces were surrounded by what appeared to be leaves, but she couldn't make out what they were.

Zale turned one of the old, tarnished knobs on the massive door. He opened it, gesturing for her to enter.

Grey curiously, but hesitantly, stepped in, immediately feeling the cold air swirl around them. She expected it to be dark, but instead, she was greeted by the warm glow of lit candles ensconced in the walls and along the winding staircase to her left. The large room was empty, and the marble floors and stone walls reflected the warm yellows and oranges from the flickering flames of the candles.

"Come on." He ascended the steps of the winding staircase.

Grey followed behind him, lightly touching the curved wall to give herself some perspective in the semidarkness. The cold stone was rough against her hand. Though it was cool in the house, being so close to Zale warmed her. She watched their shadows stretch on the stairs and along the walls as they climbed the staircase. She looked up and stopped.

"Are you okay?" Zale asked, his eyes following her gaze.

"I can see the stars."

"Yes," he said, smiling.

Grey was a little confused. If she was in the house, how could she see the stars?

"It's glass."

Grey looked up in awe. The stars twinkled perfectly through the glass.

They came to the top of the stairs. A wide landing stretched out before them. The marble railing continued to the right. Grey looked over and could see all the way down to where she came from. To the left were towering black doors that Zale effortlessly pushed open for Grey. He invited her in, gesturing with his eyes. The black marble floors matched the black marble pillars that supported a roof of what appeared to be intertwining, flowering vines. As they walked, the roof disappeared, and she saw the open sky.

"Is this where you live?"

"Not really."

Not really? What does that mean? "Where do you live?" she asked softly.

"Here." He smiled at her.

"You're not going to tell me, are you?" She wasn't going to get a straight answer out of him. Grey looked at him for a moment, and then smiled.

Zale smiled back at her.

Grey continued to look around. Unusual trees with lavender and black-streaked trunks had pushed themselves up through the floor. Their branches gave way to shimmering black leaves, reaching for the sky. Fallen flower petals were strewn upon the floor, and as she walked across, she realized it was a big balcony that overlooked the sea. She looked out over the ocean and saw the Copper Moon.

"The moon," she said, smiling.

"The Copper Moon." Zale breathed in her ear. "It's beautiful."

"It is. It's freedom," Zale said, and moved to her side.

Grey placed her hands on the railing, taking in the magnificent view. The temperature outside was perfect, and there was a gentle breeze blowing through her hair. She wanted to look at Zale, but she was too nervous. She wasn't sure what to do next, and she couldn't think of anything to say. She looked down and saw that his hand was on the railing, very close to hers. Her breathing quickened. Would he hold her hand again? The thought made her lips quirk.

"So, what do you think?" he asked.

"It's beautiful," she said. "Where are we?"

"We're here."

"Where's here?"

"This is where I go to think."

Grey had been avoiding his gaze. She wanted to look at him, but she didn't want him to know she was looking. "Oh."

"You see, we are more alike than you know." He reached for her hand and covered it with his.

"What do you mean?"

"You go on your deck to think, and I come here."

Grey smiled and lowered her head.

"I've never taken anyone here before."

"You haven't?" She stole a quick glimpse of him, making

her heart flutter even faster.

Zale shook his head.

"Why me?" she asked, softly.

He looked out over the sea.

Grey watched as he raised his face to meet the gentle breeze, allowing it to blow his hair away from his face. She noticed how long and black his lashes were, and his skin was flawless, like porcelain. The silence made her feel uncomfortable. She shifted her weight.

"You're very special, Grey."

She didn't know how to respond. She looked down at her hand in Zale's as he caressed it.

"You are special in ways you don't even know about. You have the power to free me."

Power? What was he talking about? She was just a seventeen-year-old girl trying to figure out life. "You are free."

Zale smiled. "Not as free as you think."

"I'm just me." She shrugged her shoulders.

"And that is one of the reasons you are so special." He turned his attention away from her hand and looked into her eyes. "I will give you something, and you will give me something . . . an eternal gift."

Grey looked away. She could feel him looking at her. She had no idea what he was talking about, but he made her feel the way no one had before, and she liked it.

Zale watched Grey as she looked out over the ocean. This one was a mystery to him. She was a mere human, but she intrigued him. Why? He brought her here for a reason, and he needed to follow through with his plan. He would soon be free. He took a step toward her and stopped.

Something stronger than will was preventing him from doing what he had waited so long for. Nothing ever held him back. He did exactly as he pleased when he pleased. He rarely encountered any rules in his world, and if he did, he shattered them. Why was this different? What was this? He loved to destroy with his bare hands.

He raised his hand reaching out to grab the back of her delicate neck. His fingertips barely grazing her. The thought of soaring straight up into the night sky and throwing her down with such force, her body would break, thrilled him . . . but he couldn't do it. His hand began to tremble. Weakness! His anger rose to the surface. He was the leader of the Fallen. Something as simple as destroying a meager human was never an issue for him. Zale was always in control . . . but this inner struggle he was experiencing was unknown to him. He quickly turned away and looked at his hands before clenching them tightly.

Grey turned and watched him walk to the other side of the balcony. "Zale?"

He didn't answer. She took a few steps toward him, and without turning to face her, he raised his hand explosively.

She stopped immediately and took a step back.

Centuries of emotions, bottled up emotions he never had a reason to experience, encompassed him. Being pulled in too many directions for him to bear! He couldn't break free from it. He felt lightheaded and grabbed the balcony for support as his legs buckled. What was this human doing to him?

"Zale!" Grey screamed.

The anger erupted. He roared as he fell to his knees, the wind picked up. Grey ran to Zale and put her arms around him. He was on the ground writhing in pain. Zale grabbed onto her tightly out of fear for what he was feeling. Something he had not felt in centuries. The dark, brooding storm clouds rolled in, and the wind howled with tremendous force. The ground convulsed, causing the marble pillars that stood solid for centuries to crack, and the structure heaved. Zale held tightly onto Grey, almost crushing her. He felt her strength, the strength she was unaware she had.

Finally, the confusion and emotions subsided. Her body felt good against his. Soft, warm, pure. They were both breathing heavily, and their bodies rose and fell in unison. Zale's confusion melted into passion, forgetting who he was and what he believed in. He was exhausted and gave into it. He held onto her and nuzzled his face in her hair. The hair he had longed to touch. It was as soft as he had imagined.

The earth calmed and the winds diminished. Petals from the flowers that hung overhead floated loftily to the floor, tumbling gently around them.

"We are more like Romeo and Juliet than you know," he whispered.

Chapter Twenty-Six

The Copper Moon still hung high in the black night sky as Zale stood with Grey on the beach outside her house. He pushed her hair out of her face, lightly brushing her cheek with his fingers. Chills ran through her.

"You haunt me with wonder." He slowly reached down, gently taking her hands in his. He looked into her eyes as he knelt on one knee in front of her.

"Did my heart love till now? Forswear it, sight! For I ne'er saw true beauty till this night." He kissed her hand, bowed his head, and placed her hand on his cheek, holding it there for a few moments. He stood up, stepping closer to her. Their bodies almost touched. "Thank you," he said, "for your strength tonight."

Grey's heart skipped. She looked up at him. He tilted his head slowly as he leaned down toward her. Her body began to tense. His lips were just about to touch hers. The wind howled around them, almost knocking her down. Zale quickly grabbed her, pulling her close to protect her as he looked up at the sky. Zale's arms were so strong yet gentle, and she could feel his strength as he held her. The clouds converged, hiding the Copper Moon, and rain poured down viciously, stinging their skin, and drenching them in a matter of seconds.

"Come on!" Zale yelled over the wind and rain, holding her hand, and running under the protection of the deck. "Are you okay?" he said, breathing heavily as he pushed her wet hair away from her face.

"Yes," Grey said, exhilarated as the water streamed down through the slats from the deck above.

He held her face in his hands, put his forehead to hers, closing his eyes for a moment. He brushed his cheek against hers until his parted lips were tenderly met with hers. They lingered for a moment. Zale stepped back. "I will see you soon."

She hesitated for a moment, confused by his abruptness. She didn't want it to end. "Okay."

"There is something on your pillow." Walking down the beach, he turned around. "You're beautiful!" he yelled, raising his arms to the sky.

Grey smiled and watched Zale until he disappeared, enveloped by the darkness.

She walked out from underneath the deck. The rain came down hard, but she was oblivious as she started up the steps. She remembered Zale left something for her on her pillow and her steps quickened until she reached her deck. She stopped and looked out over the dark ocean. She heard waves crashing on the beach. She closed her eyes, letting the rain run down her face, a smile fleeting across her lips before she turned and ran to the French doors.

Grey quietly turned the handle and stepped into her

bedroom, carefully closing the door behind her. There she stood, dripping wet, listening for any sound of Mom. She didn't hear anything. She quietly walked over to the lamp on her night table and turned it on. She looked at her pillow. There, she saw a beautiful red rose. She knelt next to her bed and looked at it. She was shivering. She quickly took her clothes off, putting them over the towel bar in the shower, and changed into her pajamas. Towel drying her hair, she sat on her bed and looked at the rose again. The leaves were perfectly shaped, and the rose was a deep, blood red color. She smiled. When did he put it on her pillow? She laid down next to the rose without touching it and stared at it. She wanted it to be just the way Zale had left it.

She didn't know how long she had been staring at the rose when her bedroom door swung open, startling her.

"Where have you been?" Michael demanded in a hushed voice.

"Michael!" Grey's heart pounded.

"Where have you been, Grey?"

"You scared me!"

"I scared you?" His voice rose. "No, you scared me! You didn't want me to leave your side at the party. You made a big deal about it, but then you just disappear." He threw his hands in the air. "When did you get home? I've been looking all over for you."

"A little while ago, I think."

"You think?"

"What's going on?" Mom asked sleepily, standing in the doorway in her pajamas.

Grey looked at Michael. Her stomach tightened. She wasn't sure whether he was going to tell Mom what she had done. Michael never got this angry. He was the levelheaded one.

Michael stared at Grey for a moment. "Nothing, Mom," he said, glaring at her. "I thought I heard something."

"Is everything alright?" she asked, looking at Grey.

"Yeah," Michael said before storming out of the room.

"Okay," she said. "I'm going back to bed."

Grey smiled as she laid in bed. She went through the events of the night. She enjoyed reliving them over and over, experiencing the same feelings as when she was actually going through it. Was the place Zale took her to real? Do places like that really exist? The beautiful path with the lanterns tucked away in the trees. The castle with the front doors that looked like they were from another time. The marble staircase that seemed to go on forever. The candles that cast their shadows on the walls and the balcony or whatever it was with the flowers on the floor. She had never seen anything like it before. It was like a fairy-tale castle . . . a dark fairy-tale castle.

"Did my heart love till now? Forswear it, sight! For I ne'er saw true beauty till this night." Did Zale tell her that he loved her? She repeated it over and over in her head. He said they were more like Romeo and Juliet than she knew. What exactly did he mean by that?

Grey had a hard time believing everything that was happening. Finally, she could connect with someone.

Shadow ran fiercely through the woods with his little ears flying in the air. The clouds that rolled in had gone and the rain had stopped. The Copper Moon shone again and lit his way as he dodged sticks, swerving left and right, jumping over the small brush that was in his path, never faltering for a second. His little legs barely touched the ground most of the time. He had to make it back to Breel. He didn't have a moment to lose. As long as the Copper Moon still hung in the sky, Grey could be in danger.

The little dog cut across the woods to the deserted beach and ran down to the water's edge, continuing on the damp sand where it was easier to run. He avoided the tiny waves that washed up on the shoreline, shifting his direction up the beach whenever one got too close. Breel's house was now in view, off in the distance, but Shadow didn't slow down. The closer he got, the more he pushed his little legs to go faster.

He approached the back of the house and could see the Surge, along with Lil, standing on the deck where the party had taken place earlier. He took a leap that propelled him onto the deck from the beach, landing on the deck.

"Shadow!" exclaimed Neema.

Shadow paced back and forth for a few seconds, trying to catch his breath. The little pup stopped. He gracefully leaned back on his hind legs, transforming into a boy with dark curly hair and big brown eyes, much younger than the others.

"She is safe," he said in a small voice, still trying to catch his breath.

"We know she is still with us. We feel her," Breel said, standing up and walking to Shadow.

Breel put his hands on Shadow's small shoulders.

"Are you okay?"

"I'm fine. I just ran from the Innocent's home. She is in bed."

"Where was she?" asked Murial.

"He took her."

"Zale?" asked Lil

"Yes," he said, still breathing heavily.

"Where did they go?"

"I'm not sure. I lost them. I followed them through the woods. He was creating a maze of paths for her that weren't there, and then they just . . . disappeared. I ran past them, but it was just woods, and they were gone. I didn't sense or feel them."

Lil put her hands to her mouth. "Oh no," said Lil with dread in her voice.

Breel clenched his jaw, turning away in anger.

"I'm sorry," said Shadow.

"It's not your fault. I'm not angry at you," Breel said. "This can only mean one thing."

"What?" asked Micah.

"He took her 'over'," Lil said, seriously. "That's why we couldn't find or sense them."

There was silence for a moment. The group looked at each other with great concern.

"He has never, in all eternity, taken any human 'over.' It is the only place where he is totally protected from everything. We can't touch him there," said Breel.

"Or help her," Neema said, anguish in her voice.

"But she is in bed, safe?" Breel asked, confused.

"Yes," replied Shadow.

Chapter Twenty-Seven

Zale walked down the beach. The waves gently washed ashore. The Copper Moon would soon be just a memory, and Zale wouldn't be able to have physical contact with Grey until the next one, which was a month away. This thought pained him. He pushed his wet hair back off his face and realized that he had walked down this beach for many years, but it looked different to him now. It was enthralling. Why hadn't he felt this before?

The only thing he wanted to think about was Grey and the time he spent with her. This feeling was new to him. While he did enjoy it, he was also very confused, unsettled, but why? He walked to the water's edge and looked out over the ocean. He wanted to run back and hold her in his arms and lay with her, touch her, kiss her, but the Fallen and the Surge would be looking for him. Her house would be the first place they would go. The Fallen would be suspicious, and he had to protect her . . . especially from Minna.

Zale suddenly heard footsteps grinding angrily in the sand behind him and immediately knew who it was. He closed his eyes. He really didn't want to deal with her right now but there was no way out of it. He would have to face her sooner or later. Later would have been better.

"You did it, didn't you?" Minna said.

"Did what?" he asked, exhausted.

"Reversed it."

Zale began walking away. "Yes."

"Where are you going?" Minna asked, furiously.

"What do you want, Minna?"

"Where have you been?" she demanded.

"It's none of your business."

"We went to Breel's boring party because you were supposed to be there," she said, following him.

Zale ignored her, unable to stop the delicious thoughts of Grey overwhelming his mind.

"Your little friend was there."

"My little friend?" he remarked flatly.

"Yeah, Grey. She disappeared. It was weird. She was at the party, and then she wasn't," Minna said with suspicion. "The Surge and her brother were looking all over for her, but they couldn't find her," she continued. "We thought you had done the happy deed but then realized you didn't because we can still sense her."

"That was what they were expecting me to do, Minna. That's why they had their little party, so they could keep an eye on her," Zale said, wanting Minna to go away.

"Well, it didn't work."

"What a shame." Zale smiled to himself. "They had a party for nothing."

"Zale! Stop!" Minna screamed as the wind picked up and waves crashed violently on the shore.

Zale stopped. He clenched his fists, trying to calm himself before turning around and facing Minna. "What?"

"You seem to have a lot on your mind," she said as the wind subsided and the ocean waves, once again, calmly caressed the shoreline.

"I do," he said, bluntly. He could see how distraught Minna was and realized he had to do something to convince her that he still had plans to destroy Grey.

"There's more fun to be had here, Minna," Zale said with a devious smile. "You see, they're playing our game now."

Minna crossed her arms and stood with her boots firmly planted in the sand, one hip thrust out to the side. "Tonight was the Copper Moon. You were supposed to destroy the Innocent!"

Zale walked toward her. "Since when do you tell me what to do?" he asked, losing his patience.

"I want to know what you are doing, Zale!"

"What I am doing?!" he shot back. "How dare you question my intentions!"

"Don't you want your freedom?" she asked, throwing her hands in the air.

His gaze softened. How loyal she had been to him for so long. Through the centuries, she was always the first by his side. She protected him and never wavered. "I do," he said.

"I don't understand why you're waiting."

"You don't have to, dear Minna." He sighed, a little sad.

"Yes, I do."

Zale looked at Minna. He thought she was so beautiful at one time.

"If she is the One, the glorious Celestial War will begin," she said, twirling around in circles, her arms outstretched.

"There will be no more humans after the Celestial War," he reminded her.

"And is that such a bad thing?" She continued to twirl, looking up at the fading night sky.

"What will our purpose be, if not to toy with humans?"

Minna stopped twirling. "To fight for all time side by side!" she said, excitedly. "Total chaos!"

"All in due time, beautiful Minna," he said, trying to keep his composure. He came up behind her and put his arms around her waist.

"Side by side," she smiled. "It will be just like old times." Minna closed her eyes, leaning her head back into him. She ran her hand up and down his bare arm slowly. They swayed back and forth as the Copper Moon poured its last light on the water.

Minna's eyes shot open in horror. She swiftly turned, roughly pushing Zale away from her with such force, he fell back in the sand.

Zale, startled, flew to his feet. She glared at him. "What is it?" Zale asked, confused.

Minna didn't answer. She pointed at Zale.

"Minna?"

"You . . . you . . ." her voice broke. "YOU ARE WET!"

Zale stiffened, looking down at himself.

Minna tried to digest what was happening, her chest

quickly rising and falling. "We don't get wet . . ." She shook her head. "Unless . . . unless . . . Zale?" Minna was devastated. She fell to her knees, her eyes filling with tears. "No! No! No! This can't be!"

Zale didn't even realize he was wet. He was so caught up in Grey.

"You . . . love . . . her!" She howled.

The wind began to envelop them, whipping sand into the air. Zale shielded his eyes with his hands.

Minna, still on her knees, bent over in the sand. "YOU LOVE HER! A HUMAN!" She tried to catch her breath. She raised her head and looked up at Zale. Her eyes were now black. She let out a violent scream as long discolored talons broke through her fingertips, her long, white hair blowing violently around her in the wind. "I knew this one was different, but I didn't want to believe it! She is human! I don't understand!"

"Minna! Stop!" he demanded, running toward her, trying to quiet her, comfort her.

She fiercely drew her clawed hand back. "Don't!" she growled. "It's a pity it rained." She seethed through gritted teeth. The waves grew, crashing loudly and angrily on the beach.

"I don't love her, Minna!"

"How dare you lie to me! You have betrayed me. You have betrayed all the Fallen!" she bellowed over the harsh winds.

"I have not betrayed anyone!" Zale yelled. "I know what I am doing!"

"You make me sick!" she shot back.

"Do you think I, the leader of the Fallen for centuries, could fall in love with a human?" Zale had never known Minna to be this angry with him before. He needed to think of something quickly.

"The rain only affects us when we love a human. YOU ARE WET!" she screamed to the sky.

"I don't care! I don't know why this is happening!" he fought back. "I am your leader!" He arrogantly reminded her. "I have stood by you throughout the centuries. Do you think I would betray you for a human?!"

Minna slowly lowered her hand. The winds subsided and the waves began to calm. She looked up at him like a hurt child. "You love her . . ." Minna said, defeated.

"I do not love her." Zale slowly walked to Minna.

"Then what is happening?"

"I don't know," he said, gently kneeling in the sand, in front of her. "I will find out though."

Minna sat back on her heels, exhausted. She stared down at the sand.

Zale knew the foundation of everything she ever believed in was fractured, if not destroyed. He had to convince Minna not to harm Grey. "Minna, we must keep this between ourselves. I need to find out who is doing this to me. To *us*. You know I have enemies."

Minna didn't look at Zale.

"You must remember, I am the only one who can destroy her, otherwise the Celestial War will never begin, and we will never fight side by side ending the Human Reign once and for all. *If* she is the One."

Minna took a deep breath. "I know this is true, but I don't like it."

"Minna, we have been through so much together. I have never failed you over the centuries when others tried to come between us many times."

There was no response from Minna.

"I will take care of her when the next Copper Moon is out." Zale reassured her. "You must believe me, Minna. Give me your word that you will not harm her."

"I give you my word," she said, finally lifting her head and looking at Zale, tears running down her face.

Grey quickly opened her eyes. She didn't know why she was awake or why her heart was racing. She was frozen with fear. Her eyes moved in the direction of the French doors. Nothing. She tried to calm herself. After a moment, she moved her hands and then her feet. She didn't remember falling asleep and was still lying on top of the bedspread next to the rose. It was not quite daybreak and night still lingered, casting an eerie, gray darkness into her room.

She looked around, confused, and saw a figure dash across the deck through the sheer curtains. She leapt out of bed. Was it Zale? She listened for the slightest sound outside. It seemed like an eternity. Silence. She quietly walked over to the doors, holding her breath. She moved one of the curtains, just enough to peek out. There was no one there . . . but there was something on the table.

It looked like a book. Grey squinted her eyes, trying to

make sure it was in fact a book. It was. Was it her copy of *Romeo and Juliet*? Zale! She quickly unlocked the doors, running out onto the deck, and looking around. No one. She walked over to the table when the warm ocean breeze caressed her body. She stopped and closed her eyes, enjoying the moment. She took a deep breath in; the events of the night flooded her mind. Suddenly, she felt cold breath on her face. In her half-awake state, she tried to figure out why this was so familiar to her. She was afraid to open her eyes. That familiar sinister laugh echoed, and she stiffened. She realized it was the same laugh she had heard in the darkness at Breel's house. She opened her eyes, hoping it was a bad dream, but instead saw Minna standing inches from her face.

Grey gasped.

Minna laughed again.

It was Minna in the dark basement. That same devious, condescending laugh.

Minna stared at her. Minna raised her head to the sky, opened her mouth, and let out an earsplitting scream that cut through Grey's body.

Grey, unconsciously, covered her ears. Quickly, she stepped back from Minna until her back was up against the house. She slid down, crouching onto the deck as the wind picked up and spiraled around them.

Minna's scream seemed to go on forever. Finally, she stopped and lowered her head. Her gaze fixed on Grey. Her once beautiful blue eyes were black.

Grey was terrified.

Minna laughed for a moment and then turned serious as

she took a few steps toward Grey. "This is just a warning," she growled in a voice that didn't seem human.

Grey closed her eyes tight. The wind stopped. She opened her eyes and found herself in bed, on top of the bedspread, in the same position as when she fell asleep. Her heart was racing, and she was breathing heavily. A dream? No, that was too real to be a dream, but she was in bed. Grey immediately got under the covers, pulling them over her head. She closed her eyes tightly wishing the thoughts of what just happened would go away.

Chapter Twenty-Eight

Grey felt something cold on her face as she slept but was too exhausted to give it much attention. In her groggy state, she couldn't imagine what it was and figured it would eventually stop. She felt it again, and this time, whatever it was trickled down her cheek to her neck. She lazily raised her hand and wiped her face. After a moment, she abruptly propped herself up on her elbows and opened her eyes to find Michael standing over her with a glass of water.

"What are you doing?" Grey said, letting her head fall back on the pillow.

"What happened to you last night?"

"What do you mean, what happened?" Grey sighed. "I want to go back to sleep, Michael."

"You left the party, and no one knew where you went."

"What time is it?" she asked, quickly putting the pillow over her head only to have Michael pull it away. "Michael," she whined.

"Tell me where you went. I was a nervous wreck, and I had to lie to Mom about it."

"Michael. Come on, let me sleep."

He dripped water on her face again.

"I went for a walk," Grey said, wiping the water away. She was too tired to get into the whole thing and hoped Michael would just go away so she could go back to sleep.

"I will pour this whole glass of water on you if you don't tell me."

She cracked one eye open. By the stern look on Michael's face, he was angry with her. He held the glass of water over her head and slowly tilted it. She watched the water reaching the rim. A small drop fell onto her face.

"Okay! Okay! I was with Zale."

Michael pressed his lips together and stared at her for a moment. "What?"

"I was with Zale. Now will you please let me go back to sleep?"

"No," Michael said firmly. "I want to know where you went. I didn't see him there."

Michael clearly was not going to go away. And, well, he did have the glass over her head. "I don't know where I went."

Michael began to tilt the glass again.

Grey rolled away from the tilted glass. "No, seriously, Michael! I don't know!"

"What do you mean, you don't know where you went?"

"I just don't," she said. The images of the night went through her mind. It was so unreal that someone would take her to a place that only existed in fairy tales.

"Grey?"

She looked at Michael who had the glass at his side.

"You scared the hell out of me. No one knew where you went!"

"I'm sorry."

"And after what we just went through with Mom! What about all that stuff you said about changing and caring about Mom?"

"I do care about Mom."

"I had to lie to her because of what you did. I don't lie to Mom." He stormed out of her room.

"Michael, wait!" Grey sat up in bed, but her brother slammed the door. She fell back on the bed. She stared at the ceiling before rolling over and seeing the red rose on the pillow. It wasn't a dream. Ever since Dad had passed, she felt like she was tightly rolled up into a tiny little ball, afraid of everything, but now she felt free. She could breathe again, and it felt really good, even though Michael was not happy with her. She was experiencing an excitement she had never felt before. She felt new and confident and was a little proud of herself for going with Zale because that was something she would never have done back home. She smiled, then gasped as she quickly sat straight up in bed. She needed to talk to Michael and get everything straightened out before she saw Mom.

She tiptoed down the hallway, trying not to make any noise. Carefully, she went down the stairs and saw Mom doing yard work out front through the large bay window. She quickened her pace through the living room and down the hall to Michael's room. She peeked in, hoping to find him, but he wasn't there. She hurried down the hallway to the kitchen, opened the sliding glass door, and stepped out onto the deck. No Michael. The hot wood burned her feet. She quickly walked to the edge and looked out onto the sand. She breathed a sigh of relief. Michael had dragged one of the lounge chairs to the end of the property just before the brush gave way to the open beach. The glare of the sun on the water made Grey wince as she shaded her eyes with her hand.

She didn't know how to apologize and didn't know if he would talk to her, but she needed to know what he told Mom so they could get their stories straight. Grey went down the steps to the lower deck and grabbed a towel that had been left on one of the lounge chairs. Taking small quick steps, she tried not to leave either foot on the scorching sand for too long.

When she reached Michael, she threw her towel on the sand, standing on it to give her feet some relief. Michael was lying on the lounge chair with a beach towel over his face. She didn't know what to say, and she really didn't want to get into what happened last night. What had happened was private. She just wanted to apologize and be done with it.

Normally, she would pull the towel off his face, but perhaps a more delicate method this time. "Michael?" she said, softly.

He didn't move.

Grey took a deep breath. This wasn't something she wanted to do; it was something she had to do. "Michael?" she said again as she gently pushed the lounge chair with her leg, causing it to sway unsteadily in the sand.

"What?" he asked from underneath the towel.

"I'm sorry." It was easier to apologize to the towel instead of his face.

"Whatever."

"Michael, I'm serious. I'm sorry."

Michael didn't reply.

"Will you please take the towel off your face and talk to me?"

"Why?"

He was not going to make this easy for her at all. "Because we need to get our stories straight for Mom."

"For Mom, or for *you*?" he emphasized the last word, the towel still over his face.

"For everybody. I have to avoid her until I know what to say."

Michael threw the towel off and sat up, taking Grey by surprise. "I'm avoiding her too, Grey. Do you think I like lying to her?"

Grey didn't say anything. She knew she deserved this.

"What happened to 'I'm so worried about Mom. I don't want to leave her,'" Michael said, mocking her. "Jeez, haven't we been through enough? Mom is all we have, and you go off somewhere, God knows where, and I'm left to deal with everything. God forbid something happened to you! Do you know what that would do to Mom? To me? It's just the three of us now, Grey!" He was angrier than she thought.

"I'm really sorry, Michael." She wasn't thinking about any of that last night. Now, hearing her brother say these things, she realized how foolish it was for her to disappear, leaving him to worry.

"You scared me. I didn't know where to look for you, and this morning, you tell me you don't even know where

223

you were?"

"Michael, I really don't know where." Guilt wracked her as she sat down on her towel, crossing her legs.

"Is that supposed to make me feel better? How could you go somewhere with a perfect stranger?"

Grey looked down. "He's not a stranger Michael . . . He's different," she said, picking up the sand in her hands and letting it fall through her fingers.

"Yeah, he's different alright."

"I'm okay, aren't I?"

"That's not the point. You made such a big deal about me not leaving your side at the party, and what did you do? You left me. Not only did you leave me, but you also *left* the party!"

Michael was right. He would never have left her. Grey didn't think about what she was doing. She was so excited to be with Zale that she didn't think of anything else . . . or anyone else.

"Who is this guy? You don't know him, and you don't even know where he took you?"

"I'm sorry. It all happened so fast."

"I bet it did."

"What's that supposed to mean?"

"It means that this guy has become more important to you than your own family. You know Breel had to drive me home because I couldn't ride two bikes back."

The bikes! Grey had forgotten about them.

"We don't even know these people, and they had to drive me home. I felt like such a jerk."

Grey avoided looking at him. "I'm really sorry, Michael.

Look, I don't know what else to say."

"We came here to have some peace after everything we've been through, after everything Mom's been through. She worked hard to make this happen for us, and you go and do something so stupid. It's just not like you. I don't even know you anymore."

Grey knew he was right.

"How do you think Dad would feel about this?" he asked, angrily.

Grey felt like she was just punched in the stomach. Her eyes welled up with tears.

"Exactly, Grey. He wouldn't be too happy."

"Hey, you two. What's going on?" Mom asked, quickly walking toward them, sitting on Michael's chair.

Michael glared at Grey, who turned away from Mom and wiped her eyes. "Nothing," he finally said.

"That sand is hot," she said lifting her feet from the sand.

No one said anything. She and Michael were looking off in different directions.

"So, you finally decided to come out on this beautiful day?" Mom joked, trying to ease the tension.

Grey smiled, not really knowing what to say.

"Well, I'm glad you two had a good time last night."

"Yeah, we did," Michael said, turning and glaring at Grey.

". . . and I'm sorry I missed you before you ran up to bed, Grey. Michael said you were exhausted."

She smiled nervously. "I was, Mom."

"I'm glad you're making friends."

She turned away from Mom and looked out over the beach.

Chapter Twenty-Nine

"Grey, are you coming or not?" Michael yelled from the beach.

"Coming!" Grey yelled before running onto the deck and down the steps.

Michael had already began walking down the beach.

"Wait up," she said as she ran and caught up with him.

"I don't want to be late. I told Breel we would be there at seven thirty."

"I know. We won't be late," she said. She wanted to tell him to slow down. It wasn't easy keeping up with him in the sand, but Michael was still angry at her disappearing act at the party, so she didn't say anything. Besides, he was being somewhat cordial to her. "So, where are we meeting them?" she asked, trying to make conversation.

"The drum circle."

"Anywhere in particular?"

"No, we'll find them."

Grey felt worse about what she did to Michael the more she thought about it. She didn't mean to hurt him. She just wasn't thinking about anyone but herself when she left with Zale. She wanted to tell Michael where he had taken her, what she had seen, but she wasn't sure how to begin. She watched Michael walk down the beach.

Finally, he looked at her. "What?"

"Nothing."

Silence.

"Don't disappear on me tonight," he said as he looked away.

"I won't."

He looked at her again. She was staring at him. "What?"

"Nothing."

"If you want to say something, just say it."

Grey had a knot in her stomach. It wasn't going to go away until she made up with him. "Michael, I'm *really* sorry. Look, I don't know where I was the other night, but I can tell you this . . . It was incredible."

"I'm glad you had a good time," he replied flatly.

"I did."

"You need to be careful."

"I know."

"And the fact that you don't know where you were scares me. What if he left you? How would you get home?"

Grey hadn't thought about that. "I don't know. Look, I'm sorry Michael."

"Would you even know how to get home?"

She watched her brother, who was a few steps ahead of her, and stopped walking. "Michael, it was amazing," she said.

He stopped, turned around, and looked at his sister.

"It was . . . I was in this forest with lights in the trees and a house . . . no, no, a castle that practically went up to the sky . . . and he was just really . . . unbelievable," she gushed.

Michael stared at her for a moment and sighed. "I'm glad for you, but it was stupid. Just promise me you won't do anything like that again," he said, walking back to her and hugging her.

"I promise."

"I was so scared when I couldn't find you." Michael put his arm around Grey's shoulders and walked down the beach with her.

Grey heard the faint sound of the drums in the distance, and her excitement grew. She hadn't seen Zale since the Copper Moon and was hoping he would be there. The flames from the bonfire were reaching for the sky, and she could smell the burning wood, which she was beginning to find comfort in.

"Don't forget to apologize to everyone for leaving the party," Michael said as they approached the crowd.

"I won't." Grey's stomach tightened. "Are they angry with me?"

"No, they were just concerned. That's all."

What if they asked her where she went? What would she say? She didn't want them to know. "Don't tell them where I was."

"I'm not saying a word. I know nothing."

They walked around through the crowd as night fell. The flames cast ghostly shadows on the sand, which seemed to follow them when they walked. The nighttime had become exciting to Grey. It wasn't only because that was when she usually saw Zale. She liked feeling somewhat hidden, cloaked in the darkness of night.

"Michael!" a voice called.

She turned around. Breel waved at them. They walked over to Breel, Neema, Murial, and Micah. Grey forced a smile and reached for her brother's arm.

"What?"

"I don't know," she said, shaking her head.

"Come on," he said, pulling her along. "Hey," Michael greeted the group.

"Hi," Grey said, sheepishly.

"How are you?" Neema asked.

"I'm good," Grey replied, taking a deep breath. *Just get it over with.* "I'm really sorry for leaving your party. I didn't mean to cause any problems." The apology rushed out of her.

"No problem." Breel grinned.

"Just as long as you're okay," Murial said.

"Yeah," chimed in Micah.

Grey smiled at them. *Well, that was easy.* They seemed to accept her apology and didn't seem angry with her at all. Grey looked around at the crowd, which she always found so interesting. It never seemed to be the same. She watched the sparks shoot off the flames, making them look like mini fireworks. As she stared at the fire, she saw Zale through the flickering of the flames. He was talking to his friends. Her heart began to race, and a small smile came across her lips. He looked at her, held her gaze for a moment, and looked away. Her smile faded. The excitement evaporated. He did see her, didn't he? He looked right at her.

"Are you okay, Grey?" Michael asked.

"What?" she replied, chewing her lip.

"Are you okay? You have this strange look on your face."

"Um . . . no," she said, shaking her head. "I mean, yes, I'm okay," she quickly said, trying to pull herself together. "I'm good," she said with a forced smile. She looked through the flames of the fire again, but Zale was gone.

They walked to the top of the beach. Grey followed them in a trance. She couldn't stop replaying what had just happened in her head. He saw her, but why did he look away?

"It must be great living here," said Michael.

Breel sat down on a bench and leaned back. "It's pretty cool."

Michael looked out over the beach. "I would love to live here."

Grey looked around and saw Zale standing with his friends again. They were talking to each other, laughing. He looked over at her, his laughter fading as he turned away from her. Okay, he saw her that time. What was going on? Why was he ignoring her? Minna stepped in her line of sight, blocking Zale altogether and smiling at her the way she did in her nightmare. She gasped.

"Grey?" Neema asked.

Grey clasped her hands behind her, digging her nails into her skin. "Yes?"

"Is everything okay?" Murial asked.

"I'm, I'm . . . I'm fine," she said, realizing they were all staring at her.

Michael looked at her, concerned. "Grey, do you want to go home?"

"No. It's okay."

Michael stared at his sister. Grey knew Michael was concerned about her.

"I think we're still shaken up about what happened with our mom."

"I understand," said Breel.

"Do you want to go back?" Michael asked Grey.

"Maybe we should, Michael."

"Okay."

Breel stood up. "If you need anything, just let us know."

"We will. Thanks."

The Surge watched as Grey and Michael walked down the beach.

"The Copper Moon has passed, and Zale has not acted. This is not like him at all," Breel said as he scanned the crowd. He stopped when he noticed Minna following Grey with her eyes, an evil smile on her face. She turned to meet Breel's gaze, and he immediately knew something was very wrong.

"This is not good," he said to the rest of the Surge.

Chapter Thirty

Grey lay in bed, curled up in a ball. The knot in her stomach, still gnawing at her. She didn't understand why Zale would disregard her the way he did. She was quiet on the walk home from the drum circle, and the little conversation that took place was initiated by Michael and forced on her part. She wanted to tell Michael about Zale ignoring her, but he just got over being angry with her. She didn't want him to be mad again. How could Zale be so callous after what they shared? He wasn't lying when he said those things to her. She knew what she felt from him when he touched her, held her, kissed her. She couldn't sleep. The tears burned her eyes, but she refused to let herself cry.

Then she heard a gentle tapping from the French doors. She turned her head and saw a figure through the sheer curtains. She could tell by the way the figure was standing that it was Zale. She got out of bed and tried to digest what was happening before nervously walking across the room. Her white flowing knee-length nightgown grazed her legs with each step. She slowly pulled back the curtain and peeked out to see

Zale with his back to her. Her excitement grew. She stared at him until he turned around. He smiled when he saw her. The knot in her stomach faded, her anger melting away.

He tilted his head to one side and stood there, not moving, waiting for her to come out.

Grey unlocked the door and stepped out, placing one bare foot on the deck and then the other. The gentle ocean breeze surrounded her with warmth.

Zale took a step back, inviting her to come toward him.

She pushed the door closed behind her, never taking her eyes off him. He stared at her. She didn't know what to say.

"I'm sorry I woke you," he whispered, "but I had to see you."

Grey tried to hide her excitement, but she couldn't help smiling. She felt like she had been redeemed. What they had shared meant something to him. "It's okay," she whispered back. "Is everything alright?"

"It is now," he said, smiling.

Grey tilted her head, hesitating.

"You don't understand."

"No."

"I'm sorry. There is so much involved. This has never happened to me before. It's not supposed to happen this way."

The knot in her stomach returned as she watched him pace nervously.

Grey heard a mourning dove cooing and saw the little bird perched on the deck railing. She was somehow comforted by the little bird's presence.

"I'm sorry about earlier," he said.

"You didn't even say hello," she said, softly.

He stopped pacing, took a deep breath, and turned away.

"Why?" she asked.

"I'm sorry . . . I'm so sorry." He turned to face her. "The last thing I would ever want to do is hurt you," he said, taking a step toward her, wanting to go to her, but abruptly stopping. He walked away, resting his elbows on the railing and putting his hands on his head. "My only love sprung from my only hate; too early unknown and known too late."

"Zale, are you okay?"

"Grey, do you understand how I feel about you?" he asked her with desperation in his voice.

"I think so," she said, slowly.

"No, you can't *think* so, you have to know. In your heart, your mind, your body . . . in your soul. You have to know."

Grey watched him as he spoke. He seemed so tortured. She didn't understand why something so beautiful could be so painful for him.

"There is so much I have to tell you, but it just isn't the right time . . ."

"It's okay," she said.

"Grey, I want to know everything about you," he said, stepping closer to her.

"I want to know everything about you, too."

He looked into her eyes. He wanted to hold her, but he couldn't. She took a step toward him, and he took a step back.

"What's the matter?" she asked.

"Nothing . . . Oh, there is so much that I want to tell you."

She smiled at him. "Tell me."

"So many yesterdays . . . yesterdays that I now question," he said, quietly. "I have to protect you, Grey. Please trust me."

"Protect me?"

Zale nodded sadly.

"From what?" she asked.

"I know I'm asking a lot of you, but please, just trust me."

"Okay," she said, softly.

There was silence for a moment.

"I want to hold you, but I can't."

"Why?" she said softly, taking a step toward him.

"It's just not the right time," he said, taking another step back.

The mourning dove cooed again as it perched on the railing of the deck. When she turned back around, Zale was gone.

Grey turned. The mourning dove took flight into the dark night.

The mourning dove's little heart was beating very fast as she flapped her wings and flew through the night with determination. She had to get back to Breel and the others and let them know. It appeared to her that Zale was beginning to crack. Did she hear right? Did he tell Grey that he loved her?

"My only love sprung from my only hate! Too early seen unknown and known too late!"

What was he doing to this poor girl with this "act" of his?

She approached the house and flew through an open window into the kitchen. She didn't want to waste any time by transforming until she was in front of the Surge. She landed on the living room floor and transformed into herself.

"Neema, where have you been?" asked Breel.

"I was watching Grey," she said, trying to catch her breath. "He was with her. He came to her on her deck."

"What?" Breel asked, anger rising in his voice.

"He is doing twisted things to her. Playing with her heart," she said, frantically. "He is going to break her heart before he—"

"Neema, calm down," Breel cautioned.

"He is going to have her fall in love with him, then destroy her and take her soul, and if she is the One, her soul will be no more. Why does she have to suffer? Isn't there something we can do?" Neema quickly said, her voice cracking.

No one said anything.

"She will be gone forever!" Neema cried.

"We can't let that happen, Breel," said Micah.

"Neema, what exactly did he say?" Breel asked. "If anything is to be accomplished, we have to stay calm."

"He told her that he must see her and that she didn't understand what was involved. He apologized for not talking to her at the drum circle and asked if she understood how he felt about her. He said she had to understand . . . and . . . and . . . then, I believe, he told her he loved her." Neema looked at them wide-eyed, her breathing heavy.

"He is beyond evil," Murial said, and buried her face in her hands.

"What do we do?" Micah asked Breel, who sat contemplatively looking at Neema.

"What else Neema?" Breel calmly asked.

"You're going to think I'm crazy, but he was acting weird. He was very uneasy almost like . . . he was in pain."

"Yeah, he's good at what he does," Micah replied.

"What is he doing to that poor girl?" Murial asked.

". . . And he did the oddest thing . . . He quoted Shakespeare: 'My only love sprung from my only hate! Too early seen unknown and known too late!'"

Murial and Micah looked at each other. It didn't make sense to them.

A shocked look came over Breel's face as he rose from the chair he was sitting in. The glass he was holding slipped from his hand and shattered on the marble floor, startling everyone. "This can't be," he said, stunned. It was all beginning to make sense to Breel now—Why Zale hadn't destroyed Grey on the night of the Copper Moon. "I had a gnawing feeling, but I dismissed it. I didn't believe it. I couldn't believe it . . . after all these years . . . a mortal." He was surprised at his revelation.

"What is it?" asked Murial.

"I need to find him immediately," Breel said with urgency.

Chapter Thirty-One

Zale stood teetering on the edge of Grey's roof, looking out into the black night sky. He took a deep breath. He felt alive. He thought about the events that had brought him here, and again, wondered how he had gotten to this place, which seemed so far from who he was. He didn't know what to do with the emotions. It had been centuries since he last experienced them and since then had experienced nothing but darkness, which he, in his own twisted way, fully enjoyed.

Zale also had moments of anger for letting it come to this. It wasn't the fury he was used to unleashing on the universe though. It was anger out of confusion, of not knowing how to deal with what he was feeling. Of actually being afraid to understand his emotions. He was consumed by Grey. He loved her.

How did Zale, ruler of the Fallen, wind up on a human's roof simply to watch her sleep? What was he supposed to do with these newfound feelings? He knew they could never have a normal life together. She didn't even know what he was. How would she feel when she found out? How would he tell her?

If he destroyed her, he would get the freedom he longed for, to touch humans, but she would no longer exist on earth. The Mentor would take her soul. If it turned out she was the One, she would not exist at all. Not in this world, nor Heaven or Hell. He couldn't bear the thought of her not existing here on earth. If he let her live, they would only be able to touch once a month under the Copper Moon, and he would have to protect her from the rest of the Fallen, especially Minna, who wanted the Celestial War. The Fallen would become very suspicious as to why he didn't destroy her, and it would be a constant battle with the ones who fought by his side for centuries.

What would happen to him, the leader of the Fallen? The rest of the Fallen would never respect him if he was in love with a human, the actual thing they railed against, and he would be cast out again . . . or worse. Zale couldn't imagine how painful eternity would be without Grey. Zale paced the length of the roof, tortured by the thoughts that were encompassing him. There was so much to figure out, but the only thing he wanted to do at this moment was look at her. That was something he wouldn't be denied.

Finally, not able to wait any longer, he ran to the skylight and knelt, his black coat surrounding him. There she was, sleeping in bed with the sheets pulled up just like the last time. He ran his fingers along the skylight, casting a shadow across her face as if he were touching her, his head tilting to the right as he did this. *It was the closest thing to touching her without harming her.* He lowered his gaze and turned his head slightly. After a moment, he slowly pulled his hand away from the skylight.

Someone was on the roof with him.

"Again, Zale?" taunted Breel, who stood a few feet behind him.

Zale pursed his lips. He turned to face Breel, smiling at him. "Nothing to do, Breel?"

Breel chuckled at this.

"How did you find me?" Zale asked.

"You are not hard to find these days."

Zale stood blocking the skylight as if he were a knight standing between his princess and the enemy, his long black coat blowing in the breeze.

"You are haunted by her."

Zale scoffed. "I continue my plan for her."

Breel folded his hands together and lowered his head. "Hmm, mmm. How does watching her fall into your plan of destruction?"

"I'm not going to answer your meaningless questions," said Zale. He felt Breel was wasting his time. He wanted to look at Grey, not do this dance of words with him.

"Have you given any thought to the fact that Grey may be the One?"

Zale's body tensed. "She may *not* be the One," Zale said calmly.

"True, but even if she isn't . . . don't you want your freedom to touch? Surely, that is what you've wanted for a long time. If she is the One, she is the one Innocent soul you need so you can finally unleash the fury of Heaven and Hell, wiping out what you hate the most . . . *humans*," Breel said, glancing at Zale.

Zale ignored him.

"Tell me," Breel asked, "is this hell for you, only being allowed to look at her?"

"Hell for me?" Zale laughed. "No, this is fun. Hell for me is your world."

"So, why haven't you?"

"Why haven't I what?" he asked, feigning naïveté.

"Don't you have a war to start?"

"We do not know if she is the One. Besides, I'm having too much fun right now . . . Fun I haven't had in years," Zale said, smiling. "If the War is a possibility, the War can wait."

"For someone who hates living among humans, they are also your reason for amusement, aren't they?"

"Only when I'm making them miserable."

"Or creating a façade so others think you are making them miserable."

"What do you mean?" Zale asked defensively.

"'My only love sprung from my only hate! Too early seen unknown and known too late!'"

In an instant, Zale was inches from Breel's face, his eyes as black as the night. Breel didn't waiver. "How dare you toy with me," he said in a low, vicious voice.

Breel smiled. "I thought you liked games."

"We have known each other too long. If you have something to say, then say it."

"She captured your attention. You know, at first, I didn't believe it, but the more I thought about it, the more it made sense. You thrive off her strength, and the fact that she is human intrigues and challenges you like nothing or no one else has for centuries. You have been bored, Zale, haven't you?"

"How dare you say that!"

"Ah, but she was able to touch the *Book of Eternity*," Breel said, turning his back on Zale, walking slowly away.

"Because she is an Innocent," said Zale. "She is my freedom, possibly in more than one way, and she will be destroyed,"

"The want for power is your downfall, and through power you feel greater than everyone . . . But that is why you are where you are! Cast out, unable to touch humans. Your existence is unique. You have been forced to have no physical human contact. You are a freak!"

"SHUT UP!" Zale growled.

Breel turned to Zale. "You love her!"

"Watch your words," Zale warned.

"I feel it."

"You feel nothing," Zale said, a smirk on his face.

"You love the one you must destroy to get what you've waited centuries for. So, you will get your freedom and the one you love will no longer exist. Maybe you will get your Celestial War too, but there will be no more humans for you to play with. Ironic." Breel's tense look softened, and a smirk came across his lips. "I don't know which punishment is worse."

Zale was unconsciously looking through the skylight, staring at Grey.

"You cannot stop yourself from looking at her."

He couldn't stop himself. He was drawn to her and wanted to be with her.

"You are becoming predictable . . . and that can be dangerous for you."

"I will never be predictable," Zale said almost to himself, as he continued to look at Grey sleeping peacefully.

"You are cracking . . . just a little . . . but you are cracking."

Zale ignored Breel.

"I was confused, baffled if you will. I asked myself, 'Why is he waiting? What does he want from her?' Then I realized, and it was so simple. So pure. So very . . . *human*. You want time . . . time with the Innocent."

"Breel is right," Minna said coldly, as she walked out of the darkness. "You would give it all up for a human."

Zale swiftly turned around. "Minna," he said through clenched teeth. How long had she been there?

"You lied to me, Zale. You told me you didn't love her . . . but you do," Minna said, barely able to get the words out as she walked toward him. "I knew it on the beach. I just didn't want to believe it. I've loved you for so long that I couldn't believe in anything else."

Breel took a step back getting out of their way.

"What are you doing here?" Zale asked angrily.

Minna stared at Zale. "I am doing what I need to do."

"There is nothing you *need* to do."

"You were on your knees . . ." Minna said, in total disbelief, ". . . for a human," she continued, disgusted.

"I was on my knees for no one but myself," he replied, flatly.

"What is happening to you? I don't understand!"

"You don't have to."

"I do need to understand. You lied to me on the beach!"

Her anger grew. "This is madness! You are Zale, leader of the Fallen. You have made up history, set a precedent for all others to follow. You gave us, the outcasts, a place to be. We didn't have to conform or follow everyone else or live by anyone else's rules because of you . . . Now you are taken with a human? The mere cause of our misery!"

"Enough!" Zale growled.

"You told me I had nothing to worry about!"

". . . and you don't, Minna," he said in a low voice turning away from her.

"Stop lying to me! I felt your wanting for her tonight at the drum circle. She is a human! You hate humans!" she said, her glossy eyes jet black.

"I do hate humans. This is all part of my plan. I'm having fun. So rarely do we get to have this kind of fun," he said, smirking.

"Why didn't you destroy her on the night of the Copper Moon, when you had the chance?" Minna demanded.

"I do not have to answer to you!" Zale shot back.

"You weren't at the party. Where were you?"

"We already had this conversation."

"He took her across," Breel interjected.

Zale immediately turned. How did he know? "I DID NO SUCH THING!" he roared, his eyes a deathly black.

Minna was silent. She stared at Zale in disbelief.

Breel quietly stepped back, fading into the darkness.

"You were with her?" It was all coming together for her now. "That's why she disappeared, and you weren't there." Minna began to stomp as she paced on the roof. Her combat boots scorching the roof with every step.

"What are you doing?" Zale asked, clenching his jaw.

"*What I want,*" she said, eyes locked on Zale.

"You will wake her!"

Minna smiled. "So?"

"Stop it!"

Minna ignored Zale and continued to stomp on the roof, staring at him defiantly.

"I am warning you!"

She continued to do as she pleased. "You are warning me?"

Zale glided across the roof with lightning speed. He grabbed Minna by the throat, pinning her up against the trunk of a tree that grew against the house and ascended into the sky. "How dare you disobey me?" he said through his jagged, stained teeth, his eyes wide with anger.

"How can you do this to me?" she asked.

"You are out of control, Minna. First you try to destroy an Innocent, and now this?"

"I am trying to protect you."

He tightened his fingers around her throat. His long, dagger-like talons almost breaking her delicate skin. "You defy me."

"I would never hurt you, but you have forgotten that." She struggled to speak through his grip. "What if it's a trap?"

"If it was a trap, I would know."

"You wouldn't. You are blind!"

Zale tightened his grip. His talons pierced the surface of her skin, drawing blood.

"Look what you are doing! Centuries we have been

together . . . we have protected each other," she choked through her words. She looked into his black eyes and knew at that moment she had lost him. She screamed to the sky, arching her back against the tree.

Zale lifted her up and threw her down on the roof. She immediately lifted her head and looked at Zale. She bared her once perfect teeth. now elongated and pointy. Ferociously, she rose into the night, releasing a savage scream, her three sets of wings splitting through her skin and tearing through her clothing. Her hands were now discolored, and her nails were now talons. Suspended in air, she looked down at Zale as a single tear ran down her face, veins pulsating under transparent skin. All was quiet except for the palm trees that rustled in the angry wind her rage had created.

"How could you do this to me?" she asked, in a guttural voice. "You betrayed me. You betrayed all of us!"

"I have not!" he said, looking directly at her.

"How can you look into my eyes and lie? Do you think after all this time I do not know you well enough to tell when someone has affected you? I just couldn't believe it, but now . . . I know it's true." Minna hovered there for a moment, waiting for a response.

Zale was silent.

"Enough with the games. If you cannot think clearly, then I must do what needs to be done. I will protect you from making a grave mistake."

"Minna, do not do this!"

"It is time," she said, spreading her grand wings.

"It is time when I say it is time!" Zale shot back. "How

dare you think of defying me!"

"You know I will not destroy her because the thought of her existing on a celestial level disgusts me, but I can come close enough to make her realize what a painful death would be like!" She swooped down along the back of the house to Grey's deck.

Zale ran to the edge of the roof, enraged.

Chapter Thirty-Two

Grey was woken up by a loud thud that shook the house. She sat up groggily, steadying herself, and listened. She got out of bed and walked to the French doors. Her hands tightly grasped the silver knobs. She didn't know exactly what had woken her up out of a beautiful sleep, but whatever it was, it was coming from outside. The roof to be exact. She looked up at the skylight and saw the darkness illuminated by the stars. Nothing out of the ordinary.

She turned the knobs and opened the doors cautiously, taking a step out onto the deck. She was caught off guard by the strong wind that immediately blew against her, causing her nightgown to cling to her body. She looked up as something very large swooped down past her. Grey quickly jumped back into her room, pulling the doors shut and locking them, her hands trembling. She leaned her back against the doors and listened as her heart raced. She heard a screech and slowly turned around.

Through the sheer curtains, she saw a figure drop onto the deck. It was Zale! He had his back to her, but she knew it was him. She quickly unlocked the doors and stepped out, fighting the strong winds. The creature swooped down toward Grey, letting out an angry cry. Her eyes widened as it came toward her, and just as it was going to grab her with long, sharp talons, Zale jumped up on the table and pushed the creature with such force that it tumbled into the night sky, screaming.

Grey crouched down in the corner of the deck and closed her eyes as the wind whipped around her. When she could no longer hear the creatures' awful screaming, she opened her eyes slowly. The creature was gone.

What had just happened, and what was coming after her? She didn't get a good look at whatever it was because it was so dark. The only thing she was sure of was that it was flying, and it was big. The pounding of her heart was deafening.

She lifted her head to see Zale still with his back to her, looking up at the sky. The wind subsided. She was curled up in a ball with her knees to her chest and her arms wrapped around her legs, shaking. She tried to calm herself. "Zale?" Grey said, her voice trembling.

Zale didn't say anything. Instead, he put his finger up to quiet Grey. She did not move. He lowered his hand to his side and stood, looking at the night sky. Quiet, eerie . . . Then, from above, out of the darkness, the creature ferociously flew at Zale, knocking him down onto the table.

"Zale!" Grey screamed, trying to withstand the strong winds pushing her back against the house.

Zale was immediately on his feet, unfazed by the violent winds. He jumped onto the deck railing with graceful ease, raising his hands to the sky. There, he screamed. The wind picked up speed, the trees creaking as they bent to their limits. The deck groaned and swayed. Grey lost her footing and fell onto the deck. She covered her face as leaves and sand stung her body.

She heard the terrible screaming again in the distance and looked up. The creature flew at Zale with tremendous speed. He stood stoically, his neck outstretched, baring his teeth, now long and pointy.

Grey frantically wondered why he wasn't moving. The creature was headed for Zale, it's great wings cutting through the air with ease. Just as it was inches from Zale, Grey ran and grabbed him, pulling him out of its reach. Instantly, Grey felt her hands burning as they tumbled onto the deck. The creature let out an ear-piercing cry that was so powerful, it reverberated right through Grey's body, and she thought she would explode.

The creature turned around, swooping down within an inch of her with a force so strong that Grey was thrown across the deck. Then it stopped immediately above Zale, who was face down on the deck.

"WHAT HAVE YOU DONE!?" the creature cried out in a rage over the wind, as tears ran down its face.

Grey looked up at her, horrified, realizing it was Minna. But what was she?! Grey was forced to take her eyes off Minna for a moment and look down at her hands. The burning was so intense that it was making her faint.

"You are not even the One!"

Minna pointed a long brown talon at Zale and screamed

to the sky. Her hair swirled around her as if she was underwater. "What have you done to us?!"

Grey quickly crawled to Zale, fighting the wind, and kneeled next to him, wrapping her arms around his body. The burning in her hands was getting worse and beginning to make her sick to her stomach and weak.

"Zale!" she screamed.

He lay there, his face hidden.

"Zale!" She covered him with her body, wanting to protect him from Minna and whatever it was that was happening.

He slowly turned to face her. She gasped and pulled away when she saw his black eyes and long, pointy teeth. A tear ran down his transparent cheek as he quickly turned away to hide his horrific appearance.

At that moment, Minna rushed past them with such force that Grey was thrown down on the deck, hitting her head.

Chapter Thirty-Three

rey found herself running down a wooded path. It seemed familiar, yet it frightened her. She was overwhelmed with the feeling she was being chased by something or someone, but every time she turned around, there was no one there. Her breathing was heavy, and she was beginning to feel weak. She wasn't sure how much longer she would be able to run but knew she couldn't stop. She ran off the path into the woods, thinking that maybe it would be better, cooler. The brush was dense, and she quickly realized she had made a mistake but she simply didn't have the strength to go back.

She moved deeper and deeper into the woods, constantly scraped by the brush and tree limbs. She was hot, almost feverish, and lightheaded. She stopped and rested against a tree, trying to catch her breath, but she couldn't. She couldn't stop for long, and she started running again, wiping the perspiration from her face. The hair on the back of her neck began to rise. She turned around.

Nothing.

She bolted again, looking behind her as she went. She

turned back in the direction she was running and was hit by a low hanging tree branch.

Grey quickly sat up, gripping the sheets, gasping for air. She looked around, confused, and then relieved to find she was in bed. The sun poured through the French doors, and she raised her hand to shield her eyes from the bright light. The back of her hand lightly grazed her forehead. She winced and quickly pulled her hand away. She carefully touched her forehead with her fingers, feeling a bump. Her fingers were aching, and she pulled her hand away. Her hand was red. She looked at her other hand and it was red too. Suddenly, she realized how uncomfortably warm she was.

The events of the night before came back to her. Was it real? It had to be. She looked at her hands again. Flashes going through her mind: Minna, but it wasn't Minna. She was different. She didn't have perfect skin or hands or teeth. She had wings! She flew! And Zale . . . what was happening?!

Grey was startled by a knock at her door.

"Are you okay?" Michael asked before entering. "Mom wanted me to check on you," he said, opening the door and poking his head in.

She stared at him, still trying to process what had happened last night.

"Grey, it's three thirty in the afternoon. Do you feel okay?"

She carefully slid her hands underneath the sheets. "Fine . . . I'm fine."

"You slept the day away."

She just stared at him.

"It's so hot in here." He checked the thermostat. "Did

you turn the air conditioning off?"

She stared at the sheets and didn't answer him.

"It's set to sixty-eight. That's weird. It must be broken."

"I'll be down soon, Michael."

"Okay, sleepyhead," he said, closing the door.

Grey sat on the edge of the bed. She looked at her feet, which were dangling a few inches from the floor, mesmerized by their slow circular movement. She watched them until they came to rest. They almost felt like they weren't a part of her body.

She was so tired, but something was pushing her to get up. She stepped on the hardwood floor, expecting to feel the cool wood under her feet, but instead, it was hot. She had the sensation that she was floating.

What was happening to her? She steadied herself and went into her bathroom where she looked at herself in the mirror. She looked paler than usual, but then again, she wasn't feeling great. She tried to turn on the faucet so she could splash cold water on her face, but her hands were so sore that she couldn't. She looked at her hands again and noticed they were redder than before. There was a part of her that wanted to panic, but the sheer exhaustion she was experiencing wouldn't allow her too. She used her elbow to turn on the faucet and carefully put her hands under the cold water, expecting to feel relief, but there wasn't any. She splashed the cold water on her face letting out a long sigh before walking out of her bathroom without drying her face or hands. She carefully got dressed, which took her longer than she realized because when she looked outside the sun was beginning to set.

Something continued to push her out the French doors and down the beach. Where was she going? She had no idea. It was as if something or someone was calling to her, guiding her, and she was totally trusting of it . . . whatever "it" was. The sound of the ocean seemed so distant, and though the sun was half below the horizon, she still felt its heat.

She turned into the woods. She had never noticed this path before. She heard a familiar screech off in the distance that scared her, but she wasn't sure why. Once she was under the cover of the trees, she felt a coolness that was comforting for the moment and the deeper she went the cooler it got, except for her hands, which were beginning to throb. She heard the crunching of the leaves in slow motion under her feet, as she continued through the woods, not of her own will. She felt something familiar up ahead but wasn't sure what it was. She moved toward it.

Grey found herself at an impasse. The screeching seemed closer now, yet she could tell it was coming from far away. The twisted black tree limbs and brush were so dense that she didn't see a way through, but she felt like she had gone through here before. She slowly lifted her throbbing hand, carefully touching the shiny leaves of a bush.

The immediate pain she felt caused her to close her eyes and wince. When she opened her eyes, she stood before that beautiful place Zale had taken her. The lanterns were still in the trees with black butterflies gracefully gliding through the quiet dusk.

There was something different this time, though. She looked around, trying to figure it out. Everything was darker, yet things appeared more clearly than before. The foliage, what was left of it, wilted and turned black. Though there was something very eerie about it, she felt calm and comforted. The feeling of being drawn began again, someone was pulling at her in her dream state. She continued down the path, walking faster now for she believed Zale was calling her. Past the little stone benches, she went until she came to the beautiful, foreboding structure in her sweet dreams.

Grey looked up at the sky. Dusk was turning into night. She heard a creaking sound and saw the iron gates to the house slowly opening before her. Exhausted, she stumbled toward them. They were just as she had remembered them, with shapes of little creatures with twisted faces surrounded by leaves, but now she could see them clearer. The twisted faces were those of angels and the leaves were actually wings. Why hadn't she been able to see them before?

She reached out to open the second set of doors grabbing the big black knob before quickly pulling her hand away in pain. She looked at her hands and saw that they were starting to blister. The doors slowly opened, and she felt the familiar swirl of cold air encompassing her, drawing her into the house. The screeching outside pierced her ears for the last time as the doors behind her closed. Quiet. Finally. She stood a moment blinking a few times, trying to adjust her eyes to the near darkness. The cool air gave her heated body relief.

"'I dreamt my lady came and found me dead,'" someone said in a weak voice.

She quickly turned in the direction of where it came from. There, she saw what appeared to be a huddled figure on the winding, marble steps next to the wall.

Grey walked closer. "Zale?"

"You are not the One after all," he replied, softly.

"What?"

"Oh, you have no idea, Grey . . . forgive me."

"Are you okay?" she said, wanting to go and comfort him, still unable to fully see him in the shadows.

"'These violent delights have violent ends,'" he said deviously, a smile crossing his lips as he slowly raised himself and leaned against the wall, exhausted and weak.

"*Romeo and Juliet*," she said taken aback by his tone.

"You've been reading."

"What is happening?" she asked.

"Grey . . . do you know what I am?"

"What?"

"Of course, you don't. You are truly an Innocent, aren't you?"

"Zale, was last night real?"

"Unfortunately, it was."

"I don't understand."

". . . and I don't expect you to."

"Zale, what can I do?" she asked.

"There is nothing you can do. It is all about time and the decisions we make."

Grey was confused. She walked closer to him.

"Don't come any closer."

She immediately stopped. He had never used that tone with her. "I want to see you."

"Grey, there is so much I need to tell you . . . but there

may not be time. Centuries of time with no concern, and now time is to be no more."

She looked down at her hands. The blisters were getting worse.

"Your hands . . . your beautiful hands."

"It's okay," she said, "I'm worried about you."

Zale smiled. "Such an Innocent."

"Tell me what you need to tell me."

There was silence . . . then . . .

"I am not human," Zale said, slowly.

Grey's heart raced. Not human? What did he mean?

Suddenly, Zale arched his back involuntarily and gritted his teeth, trying to hide the pain that coursed through his body. He stretched his arms down to the ground as his fingers changed into talon-like claws. Zale caught his breath as the pain passed.

"Zale?" Grey said a little frightened.

"I am an angel, Grey . . . but not the kind of angel you're used to thinking of."

Grey's head began to spin. An angel? Well, that would explain the wings on Minna, but what about the horrific change?

"I'm not the innocent little cherub with the rosy cheeks, and I'm not the beautiful guardian angel with the grand, enticing wings. They are the angels everyone loves. I am Zale, leader of the Fallen."

Grey had no idea what he was talking about, and she didn't say anything.

"Destruction . . . it is what I live for . . . what I am here for," he said weakly.

"Destruction?"

He screamed through gritted teeth, which were beginning to change into their true form. Grey wanted to run to him but she was overwhelmed. His face was hidden in the darkness. She heard his labored breathing subside. "The Fallen are angels who have been cast out of Heaven. I was the second one. I was made a spectacle of . . . reduced to ashes on the ground. Lost, until I was taken under the Mentor's wing and learned how to be truly evil over time. I keep the balance of the universe, along with the others I rule over. What sets me aside from the others is I can only physically touch a human or be touched by a human without consequence, when the Copper Moon is out."

Grey thought about this for a moment. "That's why you never touched me . . . or shook Michael's hand."

Zale took a deep breath and agonizingly raised himself in the shadows. He rested the back of his head on the wall, relief on his face. "Breel is the leader of the Surge. The good angels. The ones you read about in stories."

"But why?" she asked slowly.

"Because I questioned Him. I wanted to know why humans were so important to *Him*. Why we came second. Many thought I wanted more . . . that I wanted power . . . I realize now, I just wanted to be loved, to be considered equal. I hated humans . . . that is . . . until I met you."

". . . Why me?" Grey asked slowly.

"That is what I have asked myself over and over. When you touched the *Book of Eternity* at the Crest, I knew you were special. You intrigued me. The first Innocent to ever do so in all the centuries that I have been cursed."

Confusion crossed Grey's face.

Zale smiled. "The *Book of Eternity* is where all the celestial and earthly knowledge is set down. The book has the laws of eternity and the laws of humans. The laws of Heaven and Hell and how everything came to be . . . and how everything can be no more. No Innocent human has ever been able to touch it . . . until you. That is why some thought you may also be the One."

"Angels on Sleepy Key?" Grey said with disbelief.

"Yes, angels on Sleepy Key. We are everywhere, not just here. We are constantly battling with each other for the souls of humans."

Zale's body twisted in pain.

"Zale, what's happening?!"

". . . I am dying. Life is being pulled away from me," he said before he screamed, his body convulsing. His clothes ripped apart, releasing six sets of black and grey wings.

"No!" Grey screamed.

". . . and so are you. My beautiful Grey. Your life hasn't even begun," he said with a heavy sadness in his voice. Exhausted, he laid his face down on the marble step, his wings pulled under him. "The curse was set in motion when you touched me last night," Zale said, his breathing now labored.

Grey couldn't believe what she was hearing. This was a nightmare. "But you didn't touch me. I touched you!"

"It doesn't matter."

"This is my fault!"

"It is not your fault, beautiful one . . . it is my fault. Minna tried to warn me. I didn't want to believe her. I was so taken with you. I couldn't see anything clearly . . . including how much I felt for you. Some thought you may be the One."

"The One?"

"They thought your soul would allow the Celestial War to begin."

Grey couldn't believe what she was hearing.

"Technically . . . you are my enemy . . ." He managed a small smile.

"I don't understand, Zale. This is crazy!"

"Shakespeare, my dear Grey."

"I'm not talking about that!"

"Your soul has trapped me. Trapped me between who I am and who I now want to be."

"What am I?" she asked frightened.

"You are Grey. You are a mystery. An Innocent . . . you just have the power to destroy me."

"But I don't want to destroy you." She ran to him, laying her face next to his on the marble step.

He quickly turned his face away from her and covered himself with his wings. "Do not look at me, for I am ugly to you."

Grey looked at the huddled, winged figure. The sadness she felt was overwhelming. "You are not ugly, Zale," she said, reaching out and touching his wings. "You are beautiful."

"So pure," he said.

"Please, look at me."

"I don't want to frighten you."

"You won't."

"I am not in the form you are used to seeing me in."

"I don't care."

"I am changing into my true form, never again to be able to change into my human form. I will be a hideous monster to you."

"Please, Zale." She gently tried to urge him to move his wings and look at her, but he didn't move.

Slowly, he lifted his grand wings. Grey couldn't really see the enormity of them in what was almost pure darkness. The only light that shone on them was the faint glow from the stars that came through the glass ceiling. He slowly turned his face toward hers on the marble step. Grey saw what Zale had turned into and was unfazed. She knew how good he was, and that was all that mattered to her.

"So, what do we need to do?"

Zale smiled at her. "I love you, Grey. There doesn't need to be reasons. Sometimes you just know . . . and I know."

"I love you, too," she whispered.

"You don't find me repulsive?"

"No," she said, touching his face with the back of her hand.

"You are protected here."

"Where is here?"

"You have come over, and as long as you are here, no one can harm you nor can anyone come over."

"But what is this place?"

"I call it Delvin. It is where I go to be alone. No being, earthly or celestial, can come across unless I wish anyone to . . . and I have never wished them to, until now."

Grey could see that Zale was getting weaker, and it frightened her. "Please, tell me what to do."

"I love you, Grey, like I have loved no other."

She kissed his forehead. Zale closed his eyes, letting out a sigh. "They think I am finished. I have a plan, but I need your help."

"Anything, Zale."

"The screeching you heard when you were coming to me was the Fallen calling to each other. The word is out that I am dying. I am finished."

"No! This can't be!"

Zale struggled to take a breath. "They now know that you were not the One, for if you were, though *you* touched *me*, the Earth would have opened, revealing Hell, which would have been salivating for your soul. The Souls of Fire have been waiting to be released to begin the Celestial War . . . but that didn't happen.

"You see, Grey, there are different ranks among the Fallen . . . just like in your world. While I am the leader, there are always others who want to take my place. I have been battling this for centuries. The battles come and go, and I have been undefeated. I believe you were sent by a celestial One to destroy me so they can take my place. The celestial and earthly balance will be off kilter, and there will be a battle among the Fallen to replace me. Right now my loyal followers are calling an assembly of all the Fallen to find out who did this to me. Who sent you. They will believe they are fighting to take my place as Leader. They think I will die, and that is the way I want it. I believe whoever did this to me will come forward if I am thought to be dead. They will want to be known as the one who destroyed the first and only leader of the Fallen."

Grey watched Zale as he spoke, trying to comprehend what he was telling her.

"There will be turmoil, and the earth will feel its presence. The Surge will try to intervene to keep the earthly balance, so humans are not too affected by this. They will get the Nine Orders of Angels involved to try and avoid the war."

Grey was silent. Zale struggled to lift his discolored hand, finally putting it on the cold marble step next to his face. He tried to push himself up, but he didn't have the strength.

"'When he shall die,

Take him and cut him out in little stars,

And he will make the face of heaven so fine

That all the world will be in love with night,

And pay no worship to the garish sun.

. . . Beautiful tyrant! fiend angelical!'"

Grey didn't understand what Zale had said at first . . . After a moment, a smile came across her lips.

"If you are with me, then this is not the end, my beautiful Innocent . . . this is just the beginning," he said, slowly sliding his hand closer to Grey's, until their fingertips barely touched.

Grey heard shuffling feet on the marble floor and quickly turned. There stood a cloaked figure in the faint light, its yellow eyes piercing the darkness. After a moment, the figure pulled the hood back slowly and the piercing yellow melted into a familiar, captivating blue.

Grey, stunned, slowly got up. She walked cautiously to the cloaked figure. Her eyes welled up with tears. "Dad?"

"We have a lot to do," he said.

Acknowledgments

Mom and Dad, you gave me a beautiful life. You also gave me the nickname "Happy Wanderer", which I fully embraced and eventually, it became a little "adventure" for you. Thank you for teaching me how to dream, which led to my mischievousness … and that also, became a little "adventure" for you. Thank you for your unwavering love and dedication.

Dad, when I was little, I used to wake you up before dawn on the weekends and ask you to write down the stories I had in my head. You always did this for me, never complaining. Thank you isn't enough. Mom, you took me to the library and showed me that books open magnificent worlds where anything is possible. I will always draw from your strength and love. I had the best teacher. I wish you both could have stuck around just a little bit longer. Time …there's never enough. I hope I made you proud.

Pete Konczal, thank you for sharing your love, light and that star in the sky. The music is magic, the journey, real …

sometimes too real and that, in turn, becomes the glue ... and to think, it all started with a drink.

Bodhi and Everly, you enlighten me every day. I am in awe of your wonder, resilience, kindness, and the way you see the world. Watching you grow is a gift. I need to have a conversation with Time. It needs to slow down so I may linger with you both a little longer each day. I love you to infinity and back!

Shadow, you are my first born. An angel in fur, my partner in crime. You're always up for any adventure. Thank you for never leaving my side. You know all my secrets.

Melanie Gold, thank you for helping me choose the right path when I found myself at those stinkin' forks in the road during the creation of this book. Our friendship ... worth so much more than a quarter.

Brian J. Goldberg, LA may have seeped into your veins, but thankfully, you are still a Jersey Boy. Grateful for you!

To everyone at Indigo River, thank you. You weren't afraid to take this crazy ride with me. My editor, Deborah Froese, thank you for your inspiration, guidance, and honesty.

www.ingramcontent.com/pod-product-compliance
Lightning Source LLC
Chambersburg PA
CBHW021005260626
47169CB00006B/1961